Spook Stories
Edward Frederic Benson

Edward Frederic Benson (1867 – 1940) was an English novelist, biographer, memoirist and short story writer, known professionally as E.F. Benson. His friends called him Fred.

Benson's first book was Sketches from Marlborough. He started his novel writing career with the (then) fashionably controversial Dodo (1893), which was an instant success, and followed it with a variety of satire and romantic and supernatural melodrama. He repeated the success of Dodo, which featured a portrait of composer and militant suffragette Ethel Smyth with the same cast of characters a generation later: Dodo the Second (1914) and Dodo Wonders (1921) The Mapp and Lucia series, written relatively late in his career, consists of six novels and two short stories. The novels are: Queen Lucia, Lucia in London, Miss Mapp (including the short story "The Male Impersonator"), Mapp and Lucia, Lucia's Progress (published as The Worshipful Lucia in the United States) and Trouble for Lucia. The short stories are "The Male Impersonator" and "Desirable Residences".

Spook Stories
I
RECONCILIATION

Garth Place lies low in a dip of the hills which, north, east, and west, enclose its sequestered valley, as in the palm of a hollowed hand. To the south the valley broadens out and the encompassing hills merge themselves into the wide strip of flat country once reclaimed from the sea, and now, with intersections of drainage dykes, forming the fat pasture of the scattered farms. Thick woods of beech and oak, which climb the hillsides above the house up to the top of the ridge, give it further shelter, and it dozes in a soft and sundered climate of its own when the bleak uplands above it are swept by the east winds of spring or the northerly blasts of winter; and, sitting in its terraced garden in the mild sunshine of a clear December day, you may hear the gale roaring through the tree-tops on the upper slopes, and see the clouds scudding high above you, yet never feel a breath of the wind that shreds them seawards. The clearings in these woods are thick with anemones and full-blown clumps of primroses a month before the tiniest bud has appeared in the copses of the upland, and its gardens are still bright with the red blossoms of the autumn long after the flower-borders in the village that huddles on the hill-top to the west have been blackened by the frosts. Only when the south wind blows is its tranquillity disturbed, and then the sound of the waves is heard, and the wind is salt with the sea.

The house itself dates from the beginning of the seventeenth century, and has miraculously escaped the destructive hand of the restorer. Its three low storeys are built of the grey stone of the district, the roof is made of thin slabs of the same, between which the blown seeds have found anchorage, and the broad mullioned windows are many-paned. Never a creak comes from its oaken floors, solid and broad are its staircases, its panelling is as firm as the walls in which it is laid. A faint odour of wood smoke from the centuries of fires that have burned on its open hearths pervades it, that and an extraordinary silence. A man who lay awake all night in one of its chambers would hear no whisper of cracking wood-work, or rattling pane, and all night long there would come to his listening ears no sound from outside but the hoot of the tawny owl, or in June the music of the nightingale. At the back a strip of garden has been anciently levelled out of the hillside, in front the slope has been built up to form a couple of terraces. Below, a spring feeds a small sheet of water, bordered by marshy ground set with tufts of rushes, and out of it a stream much stifled in herbage wanders exiguously past the kitchen garden, and joins the slow-flowing little river which, after a couple of miles of lazy travel, debouches through broadening mud-flats into the English Channel. Along the further margin of the stream a footpath with right-of-way leads from the village of Garth on the hill above to the main road across the plain. Just below the house a small stone bridge with a gate crosses the stream and gives access to this footpath.

I first saw the house to which now for so many years I have been a constant visitor when I was an undergraduate at Cambridge. Hugh Verrall, the only son of its widowed owner, was a friend of mine, and he proposed to me one August that we should have a month there together. His father, he explained, was spending the next six weeks at a foreign health resort. Mine, so he understood, was tied in London, and this really seemed a more agreeable way of getting through August than that he should inhabit his house in melancholy solitude, and that I should stew in town. So if the notion at all appealed to me, I had but to get the parental permission; it had already received his father's sanction. Hugh, in fact, produced Mr. Verrall's letter in which he stated his views as to his son's disposal of his time with great lucidity.

"I won't have you hanging about at Marienbad all August," he said, "for you'll only get into mischief, and spend the rest of your allowance for the year. Besides, there's your work to think of; you didn't do a stroke, so your tutor informed me, all last term, so you'd better make up for it now. Go down to Garth, and get some pleasant, idle scamp like yourself to stay with you, and then you'll have to work, for you won't find anything else to do! Besides, nobody wants to do anything at Garth."

"All right, the idle scamp will come," said I. I knew my father didn't want me to be in London, either.

"Mark you, the idle scamp has to be pleasant," said Hugh. "Well, you'll come anyhow; that's ripping. You'll see what my father means by not wanting to do anything. That's Garth."

The end of the next week saw us installed there, and never in all the first sights of the various splendours of the world that have since then been accorded to me, have I felt so magical and potent a spell as that which caught the breath in my throat when on the evening of that hot August day I first saw Garth. For a mile before the road had lain through the woods that clothe the slope above it; from there my cab emerged as from a tunnel, and there in the clear twilight, with sunset flaming overhead, was the long grey façade, with the green lawns about it, and its air of antique and native tranquillity. It seemed an incarnation of the very soul and spirit of England: there in the south was the line of sea, and all round it the immemorial woods. Like its oaks, like the velvet of its lawns, the house had grown from the very soil, and the life of the soil still richly nurtured it. Venice was not more authentically born from the sea, nor Egypt from the mystery of the Nile, than Garth was born from the woods of England.

There was time for a stroll round before dinner, and Hugh casually recounted the history of it. His forebears had owned it since the time of Queen Anne.

4

"But we're interlopers," he said, "and not very creditable ones. Before that, my people had been tenants of the farm you passed at the top of the hill, and the Garths were in possession. It was a Garth who built the house in the reign of Elizabeth."

"Ah, then you've got a ghost," I said. "That makes it quite complete. Don't tell me that there isn't a Garth who haunts the house?"

"Anything to oblige," said he, "but that I am afraid I can't manage for you. You're too late: a hundred years ago it certainly was supposed to be haunted by a Garth."

"And then?" I asked.

"Well, I know nothing about spooks, but it looks as if the haunt wore itself out. It must be tiresome, you know, for a spirit to be chained to a place, and have to walk about the garden in the evening, and patrol the passages and bedrooms at night, if nobody pays any attention to it. My forebears didn't care the least, it appears, whether the ghost haunted the place or not. In consequence, it evaporated."

"And whose ghost was it supposed to be?" I asked.

"The ghost of the last Garth, who lived here in the time of Queen Anne. What happened was this. A younger son of my family, Hugh Verrall—same name as me—went up to London to seek his fortune. He made a lot of money in a very short time, and when he was a middle-aged man he retired, and took it into his head that he would like to be a country gentleman with an estate of his own. He was always fond of this country, and came to live at a house in the village up there, while he looked about, and no doubt he had ulterior purposes. For Garth Place was at that time in the hands of a wild fellow called Francis Garth, a drunkard and a great gambler, and Hugh Verrall used to come down here night after night and thoroughly fleece him. Francis had one daughter, who of course was heiress to the place; and at first Hugh made up to her with the idea of marrying her, but when that was no use, he took to the other way of getting hold of it. Eventually, in the fine traditional manner, Francis Garth, who by that time owed my ancestor something like thirty thousand pounds, staked the Garth property against his debt and lost. There was a tremendous excitement over it, with stories of loaded dice and marked cards, but nothing could be proved, and Hugh evicted Francis and took possession. Francis lived for some years yet, in a labourer's cottage in the village, and every evening he used to walk down the path there, and standing opposite the house, curse the inhabitants. At his death, the haunt began, and then, simply it died out."

"Perhaps it's storing force," I suggested. "Perhaps it's intending to come out strong again. You ought to have a ghost here, you know."

"Not a trace of one, I'm afraid," said Hugh; "or I wonder if you'll think there is still a trace of it. But it's such a silly trace that I'm almost ashamed to tell you about it."

"Go on quickly," said I.

He pointed up to the gable above the front door. Underneath it, in an angle formed by the roof, there was a big square stone, evidently of later date than the wall. The surface of it was in contrast to the rest of the wall, much crumbled, but it had evidently been carved, and the shape of a heraldic shield could be seen on it, though of the arms it carried there was nothing left.

"It's too silly," said Hugh, "but it is a fact that my father remembers that stone being placed there. His father put it up, and it bore our coat of arms: you can just see the shape of the shield. But, though it was of the stone of the district, exactly like the rest of the house, it had hardly been put up when the surface began to decay, and in ten years our arms were absolutely obliterated. Odd, that just that one stone should have perished so quickly, when all the rest really seems to have defied time."

I laughed.

"That's Francis Garth's work beyond a doubt," I said. "There's life in the old dog yet."

"Sometimes I think there is," he said. "Mind you, I've never seen or heard anything here which is in the smallest way suggestive of spooks, but constantly I feel that there is something here that waits and watches. It never manifests itself, but it's there."

As he spoke, I caught some faint psychical glimpse of what he meant. There was something there, something sinister and malevolent. But the impression was of the most momentary sort; hardly had it conveyed itself to me when it vanished again, and the amazing beauty and friendliness of the house overwhelmingly reasserted itself. If ever there was an abode of ancient peace, it was here.

We settled down at once into a delightful existence. Being very great friends, we were completely at ease with each other; we talked as we felt disposed but if a silence fell there was no constraint about it, and it would continue, perfectly happily, till one of us was moved to speak again. In the morning for three hours or so we applied ourselves very studiously to our books, but by lunch-time they were closed for the day, and we would walk across the marsh for a swim in the sea or stray through the woods, or play bowls on the lawn behind the house. The weather, blazing hot, predisposed to laziness, and in that cupped hollow of the hills, where the house stood, it was almost impossible to remember what it felt like to be energetic. But, as Hugh's father had indicated, that was the proper state of body and mind to be in when you resided at Garth. You must be sleepy and hungry and well, but without desires or energies; life moved along there as on some lotus-eater's shore, very softly and quietly without disturbance. To be lazy without scruple or compunction but with a purring content was to act in accordance with the spirit of Garth. But, as the days went on, I knew that below this content there was something in us both that grew ever more alert and watchful for that which was watching us.

We had been there about a week when on an afternoon of still and sultry heat, we went down to the sea for a dip before dinner. There was clearly a storm coming up, but it seemed possible to get a bathe and return before it broke. It came up, however, more quickly than we had thought, and we were still a mile from home when the rain began, heavy and windless. The clouds, which had spread right across the sky, made a darkness as of late twilight, and when we struck the little public footpath on the far side of the stream in front of the house, we were both drenched to the skin. Just as we got to the bridge I saw the figure of a man standing there, and it struck me at once as odd that he should wait out in this deluge and not seek shelter. He stood quite still looking towards the house, and as I passed him I had one good stare at his face and instantly knew that I had seen a face very like it before, though I could not localise my memory. He was of middle-age, clean-shaven, and there was something curiously sinister about that lean, dark-skinned profile.

However, it was no business of mine if a stranger chose to stand out in the rain and look at Garth Place, and I went on a dozen steps, and then spoke to Hugh in a low voice.

"I wonder what that man's doing there," I said.

"Man? What man?" said Hugh.

"The man by the bridge whom we passed just now," I said.

He turned round to look.

"There's no one there," he said.

Now it seemed quite impossible that this stranger who had certainly been there so few seconds ago, could have vanished into the darkness, thick as it was, and at that moment for the first time it occurred to me that this was no creature of flesh and blood into whose face I had looked. But Hugh had hardly spoken when he pointed to the path up which we had come.

"Yes, there is someone there," he said. "Odd that I didn't see him as we passed. But if he likes to stand about in the rain, I suppose he can."

We went on quickly up to the house, and as I changed I cudgelled my brain to think when and where I had seen that face before. I knew it was quite lately, and I knew I had looked with interest at it. And then suddenly the solution came to me. I had never seen the man before, but only a picture of him, and that picture hung in the long gallery at the front of the house, into which Hugh had taken me the first day that I was here, but I had not been there since. Portraits of Verralls and Garths hung on the walls, and the portrait in question was that of Francis Garth. Before going downstairs I verified this, and there was no doubt whatever about it. The man whom I had passed on the bridge was the living image of him who, in the time of Anne, had forfeited the house to Hugh's ancestral namesake.

I said nothing about this identification to Hugh, for I did not want to put any suggestion into his mind. For his part, he made no further allusion to our encounter; it had evidently made no particular impression on him, and we spent the evening as usual. Next morning, we sat at our books in the parlour overlooking the bowling-green. After an hour's work, Hugh got up for a few minutes' relaxation, and strolled whistling, to the window. I was not following his movements with any attention, but I noticed that his whistling stopped in the middle of a phrase. Presently he spoke in rather a queer voice.

"Come here a minute," he said.

I joined him, and he pointed out of the window.

"Is that the man you saw yesterday by the bridge?" he said. There he was at the far end of the bowling-green looking straight at us.

"Yes, that's he," I said.

"I shall go and ask him what he's doing here," said Hugh. "Come with me!"

We went together out of the room and down the short passage to the garden door. The quiet sunlight slept on the grass, but there was no one there.

"That's queer," said Hugh. "That's very queer. Come up to the picture gallery a minute."

"There's no need," said I.

"So you've seen the likeness, too," he said. "I say—is it a likeness only, or is it Francis Garth? Whatever it is, it's that which is watching us."

The apparition which, from that time, we both thought and spoke of as Francis Garth, had now been seen twice. During the next week it seemed to be drawing nearer to the house that had once been its haunt, for Hugh saw it just outside the porch by the front door, and a day or two afterwards, as I sat at twilight in the room overlooking the bowling-alley waiting for him to come down to dinner, I saw it close outside the window looking narrowly into the room with malevolent scrutiny. Finally, a few days only before my visit here came to an end, as we returned one evening from a ramble in the woods, we saw it together, standing by the big open fireplace in the hall. This time its appearance was not momentary, for on our entry it remained where it was, taking no notice of us for perhaps ten seconds, and then moved away towards the far doorway. There it stopped and turned, looking directly at Hugh. At that he spoke to it, and without answer it passed out through the door. It had now definitely come inside; and from that time onwards was seen only within the house. Francis Garth had taken possession again.

Now I do not pretend that the sight of this apparition did not affect my nerves. It affected them very unpleasantly; fright, perhaps, is too superficial a word with which to describe the effect it had on me. It was rather some still, dark horror of the spirit that closed over me, not (to be precise) at the moment when I actually saw it, but some few seconds before, so that I knew by this dire terror that invaded me that the apparition was about to manifest itself. But mingled with that was an intense interest and curiosity as to the nature of this strange visitant, who, though long dead, still wore the semblance of the living, and clothed itself in the body which had long

8

crumbled to dust. Hugh, however, felt nothing of this; the spectre alarmed him as little now on its second inhabiting of the house, as it had alarmed those who lived here when first it appeared.

"And it's so interesting," he said, as he saw me off on the conclusion of my visit. "It's got some business here, but what can that business be? I'll let you know if there's any further development."

From that time onwards the ghost was constantly seen. It alarmed some people, it interested others, but it harmed none. Often during the next five years or so, I stayed there, and I do not think that any visit passed without my seeing it once or twice. But always to me its appearance was heralded by that terror of which I have spoken, in which neither Hugh nor his father shared. And then quite suddenly Hugh's father died. After the funeral, Hugh came up to London for interviews with lawyers and for the settlement of affairs connected with the will, and told me that his father was not nearly so well-off as had been supposed, and that he hardly knew if he could afford to live at Garth Place at all. He intended, however, to shut up part of the house, and with a greatly reduced household to attempt to continue there.

"I don't want to let it," he said; "in fact, I should hate to let it. And I don't really believe that there's much chance of my being able to do so. The story of its being haunted is widely known now, and I don't fancy it would be very easy to get a tenant for it. However, I hope it won't be necessary."

But six months later he found that in spite of all economies it was no longer possible to live there, and one June I went down for a final visit, after which, unless he succeeded in getting a tenant, the house would be shut up.

"I can't tell you how I dislike having to go," he said, "but there's no help for it. And what are the ethics of letting a haunted house, do you think? Ought one to tell an intending tenant? I advertised the house last week in _Country Life_, and there's been an enquirer already. In fact, he's coming down with his daughter to see the house to-morrow morning. Name of Francis Jameson."

"I hope he'll hit it off with the other Francis," I said. "Have you seen him much lately?"

Hugh jumped up.

"Yes, fairly often," he said. "But there's an odd thing I want to show you. Come out of doors a minute."

He took me out to the front of the house, and pointed to the gable below which was the shield containing his obliterated arms.

"I'll give you no hint," he said. "But look at it and make any comment."

"There's something appearing there," said I. "I can see two bends crossing the shield, and some device between them."

"And you're sure you didn't see them there before?" he asked.

"I certainly thought the surface had quite perished," I said. "Of course, it can't have. Or have you had it restored?"

He laughed.

9

"I certainly haven't," he said. "In fact, what you see there isn't part of my arms at all, but the Garth arms."

"Nonsense. It's some chance cracks and weatherings that have come on the stone, rather regular, certainly, but accidental."

He laughed again.

"You don't really believe that," he said. "Nor do I, for that matter. It's Francis: Francis is busy."

I had gone up to the village next morning, over some small business, and as I came back down the footpath opposite the house saw a motor drive up to the door, and concluded that this was Mr. Jameson who had just arrived. I went indoors, and into the hall, and next moment was standing there with staring eyes and open mouth. For just inside were three people talking together: there was Hugh, there was a very charming-looking girl, obviously Miss Jameson, and the third, so my eyes told me, was Francis Garth. As surely as I had recognised the spectre as him whose portrait hung in the gallery, so surely was this man the living and human incarnation of the spectre itself. You could not say it was a likeness: it was an identity.

Hugh introduced me to his two visitors, and I saw in his glance that he had been through much the same experience as I. The interview and the inquiries had evidently only just begun, for after this little ceremony Mr. Jameson turned to Hugh again.

"But before we see the house or garden," he said, "there is one most important question I have to ask, and if your answer to that is unsatisfactory, I shall but waste your time in asking you to show me over."

I thought that some inquiry about the ghost was sure to follow, but was quite wrong. This paramount consideration was climate, and Mr. Jameson began explaining to Hugh with all the ardour of the invalid, his requirements. A warm, soft air, with an absence of easterly and northerly winds in winter, was what he was seeking for, a sheltered and sunny situation.

The replies to these questions were sufficiently satisfactory to warrant an inspection of the house, and presently all four of us were starting on our tour.

"Go on first, my dear Peggy, with Mr. Verrall," said Mr. Jameson to his daughter, "and leave me to follow a little more leisurely with this gentleman, if he will kindly give me his escort. We will receive our impressions independently, too, in that way."

It occurred to me once again that he wanted to make some inquiry about the house, and preferred to get his information not from the owner, but from someone who knew the place, but was in no way connected with the business of letting it. And again I waited to hear some questions about the ghost. But what came surprised me much more.

He waited, evidently with purpose, till the other two had passed some distance on, and then turned to me.

"Now a most extraordinary thing has happened," he said. "I have never set eyes on this house before, and yet I know it intimately. As soon as we came to the front door I knew what this room would be like, and I can tell you what we shall see when we follow the others. At the end of the passage up which they have gone there are two rooms, of which the one looks out on to a bowling-green behind the house, the other on to a path close below the windows, from which you can look into the room. A broad staircase ascends from there in two short flights to the first floor, there are bedrooms at the back, along the front runs a long panelled room with pictures. Beyond that again are two bedrooms with a bathroom in between. A smaller staircase, rather dark, ascends from there to the second floor. Is that correct?"

"Absolutely," said I.

"Now you mustn't think I've dreamed these things," he said. "They are in my consciousness, not as a dream at all, but as actual things I knew in my own life. And they are accompanied by a feeling of hostility in my mind. I can tell you this also, that about two hundred years ago my ancestor in the direct line married a daughter of Francis Garth and assumed her arms. This is Garth Place. Was a family of Garth ever here, or is the house simply named after the village?"

"Francis Garth was the last of the Garths who lived here," said I. "He gambled the place away, losing it to the direct ancestor of the present owner; his name also was Hugh Verrall."

He looked at me a moment with a puzzled air, that gave his face a curiously sharp and malevolent expression.

"What does it all mean?" he said. "Are we dreaming or awake? And there's another thing I wanted to ask you. I have heard—it may be mere gossip— that the house is haunted. Can you tell me anything about that? Have you ever seen anything of the sort here? Let us call it a ghost, though I don't believe in the existence of such a thing. But have you ever seen any inexplicable appearance?"

"Yes, frequently," I said.

"And may I ask what it was?"

"Certainly. It was the apparition of the man of whom we have been speaking. At least, the first time I saw it I at once recognised it as the ghost—if I may use the word—of Francis Garth, whose portrait hangs in the gallery you have correctly described."

I hesitated a moment, wondering if I had better tell him that not only had I recognised the apparition from the portrait, but that I had recognised him from the apparition. He saw my hesitation.

"There is something more," he said.

I made up my mind.

"There is something more," I said, "but I think it would be better if you saw the portrait for yourself. Possibly it will tell you more directly and convincingly what that is."

We went up the stairs which he had described without first visiting the other rooms on the ground floor, from which I heard the voice of Hugh and his companion. There was no need for me to point out to Mr. Jameson the portrait of Francis Garth, for he went straight to it, and looked at it for a long while in silence. Then he turned to me.

"So it's I who ought to be able to tell you about the ghost," he said, "instead of your telling me."

The others joined us at this moment, and Miss Jameson came up to her father.

"Oh, Daddy, it's the most delicious home-like house," she said. "If you won't take it, I shall."

"Have a look at my portrait, Peggy," said he.

We changed partners after that, and presently Miss Peggy and I were strolling round the outside of the house while the others lingered within. Opposite the front door she stopped and looked up at the gable.

"Those arms," she said. "It's hard to make them out, and I suppose they're Mr. Verrall's? But they're wonderfully like my father's."

After we had lunched, Hugh and his proposed tenant had a private talk together, and soon after his visitors left.

"It's practically settled," he said as we turned back into the hall again after seeing them off. "Mr. Jameson wants a year's lease with option to renew. And now what do you make of it all?"

We talked it out lengthways and sideways and right way up, and upside down, and theory after theory was tried and found wanting, for some pieces seemed to fit together, but we could not dovetail them in with others. Eventually, after hours of talk, we reasoned it out, granting that it was all inexplicable, in a manner that may or may not commend itself to the reader, but seems to cover the facts and to present what I may perhaps call a uniform surface of inexplicability.

To start then at the beginning, shortly summing up the facts, Francis Garth, dispossessed, possibly with fraud, of his estate, had cursed the incomers and apparently haunted it after his death. Then came a long intermission from any ghostly visitant, and once more the haunt began again at the time when I first stayed here with Hugh. Then to-day there had come to the house a direct descendant of Francis Garth, who was the living image of the apparition we had both so constantly seen, which, by the portrait, was also identified with Francis Garth himself. And already, before Mr. Jameson had entered the house, he was familiar with it and knew what was within, its staircases and rooms and corridors, and remembered that he had often been here with hostility in his soul, even as we had seen hostility on the face of the apparition. What, then (here is the theory that slowly emerged), if we see in Francis Jameson some reincarnation of Francis Garth, purged, so to speak, of his ancient hostility, and coming back to the house which two hundred years ago was his home, and finding a home there once more? Certainly from that

12

day no apparition, hostile and malevolent, has looked in through its windows, or walked in its bowling-alley.

In the sequel, too, I cannot help seeing some correspondence between what happened now and what happened when in the time of Anne Hugh Verrall took possession: here was what we may think of as the reverse of the coin that was hot-minted then. For now another Hugh Verrall, unwilling, for reasons that soon became very manifest, to leave the place altogether, established himself in a house in the village, even as his ancestor had done, and amazingly frequent were his visits to the home of his fathers, which was for the present the house of those whose family had owned it before the first of his forefathers came there. I see, too, a correspondence, which Hugh certainly would be the last to pass lightly over, in the fact that Francis Jameson, like Francis Garth, had a daughter. At that point, however, I am bound to say that strict correspondence is rudely broken, for whereas Hugh Verrall the first had no luck when he went a-wooing the daughter of Francis Garth, a much better fortune attended the venture of Hugh Verrall the second. In fact, I have just returned from their marriage.

II

THE FACE

Hester Ward, sitting by the open window on this hot afternoon in June, began seriously to argue with herself about the cloud of foreboding and depression which had encompassed her all day, and, very sensibly, she enumerated to herself the manifold causes for happiness in the fortunate circumstances of her life. She was young, she was extremely good-looking, she was well-off, she enjoyed excellent health, and above all, she had an adorable husband and two small, adorable children. There was no break, indeed, anywhere in the circle of prosperity which surrounded her, and had the wishing-cap been handed to her that moment by some beneficent fairy, she would have hesitated to put it on her head, for there was positively nothing that she could think of which would have been worthy of such solemnity. Moreover, she could not accuse herself of a want of appreciation of her blessings; she appreciated enormously, she enjoyed enormously, and she thoroughly wanted all those who so munificently contributed to her happiness to share in it.

She made a very deliberate review of these things, for she was really anxious, more anxious, indeed, than she admitted to herself, to find anything tangible which could possibly warrant this ominous feeling of approaching disaster. Then there was the weather to consider; for the last week London had been stiflingly hot, but if that was the cause, why had she not felt it before? Perhaps the effect of these broiling, airless days had been cumulative. That was an idea, but, frankly, it did not seem a very good one, for, as a matter of fact, she loved the heat; Dick, who hated it, said that it was odd he should have fallen in love with a salamander.

She shifted her position, sitting up straight in this low window-seat, for she was intending to make a call on her courage. She had known from the moment she awoke this morning what it was that lay so heavy on her, and now, having done her best to shift the reason of her depression on to anything else, and having completely failed, she meant to look the thing in the face. She was ashamed of doing so, for the cause of this leaden mood of fear which held her in its grip, was so trivial, so fantastic, so excessively silly.

"Yes, there never was anything so silly," she said to herself. "I must look at it straight, and convince myself how silly it is." She paused a moment, clenching her hands.

"Now for it," she said.

She had had a dream the previous night, which, years ago, used to be familiar to her, for again and again when she was a child she had dreamed it. In itself the dream was nothing, but in those childish days, whenever she had this dream which had visited her last night, it was followed on the next night by another, which contained the source and the core of the horror, and she would awake screaming and struggling in the grip of overwhelming nightmare. For some ten years now she had not experienced it, and would have said that, though she remembered it, it had become dim and distant to her. But last night she had had that warning dream, which used to herald the visitation of the nightmare, and now that whole store-house of memory crammed as it was with bright things and beautiful contained nothing so vivid.

The warning dream, the curtain that was drawn up on the succeeding night, and disclosed the vision she dreaded, was simple and harmless enough in itself. She seemed to be walking on a high sandy cliff covered with short down-grass; twenty yards to the left came the edge of this cliff, which sloped steeply down to the sea that lay at its foot. The path she followed led through fields bounded by low hedges, and mounted gradually upwards. She went through some half-dozen of these, climbing over the wooden stiles that gave communication; sheep grazed there, but she never saw another human being, and always it was dusk, as if evening was falling, and she had to hurry on, because someone (she knew not whom) was waiting for her, and had been waiting not a few minutes only, but for many years. Presently, as she mounted this slope, she saw in front of her a copse of stunted trees, growing crookedly under the continual pressure of the wind that blew from the sea, and when she saw those she knew her journey was nearly done, and that the nameless one, who had been waiting for her so long was somewhere close at hand. The path she followed was cut through this wood, and the slanting boughs of the trees on the sea-ward side almost roofed it in; it was like walking through a tunnel. Soon the trees in front began to grow thin, and she saw through them the grey tower of a lonely church. It stood in a graveyard, apparently long disused, and the body of the church, which lay between the tower and the edge of the cliff, was in ruins, roofless, and with gaping windows, round which ivy grew thickly.

At that point this prefatory dream always stopped. It was a troubled, uneasy dream, for there was over it the sense of dusk and of the man who had been waiting for her so long, but it was not of the order of nightmare. Many times in childhood had she experienced it, and perhaps it was the subconscious knowledge of the night that so surely followed it, which gave it its disquiet. And now last night it had come again, identical in every particular but one. For last night it seemed to her that in the course of these ten years which had intervened since last it had visited her, the glimpse of the church and churchyard was changed. The edge of the cliff had come nearer to the tower, so that it now was within a yard or two of it, and the ruined body of the church, but for one broken arch that remained, had vanished. The sea had encroached, and for ten years had been busily eating at the cliff.

Hester knew well that it was this dream and this alone which had darkened the day for her, by reason of the nightmares that used to follow it, and, like a sensible woman, having looked it once in the face, she refused to admit into her mind any conscious calling-up of the sequel. If she let herself contemplate that, as likely or not the very thinking about it would be sufficient to ensure its return, and of one thing she was very certain, namely, that she didn't at all want it to do so. It was not like the confused jumble and jangle of ordinary nightmare, it was very simple, and she felt it concerned the nameless one who waited for her.... But she must not think of it; her whole will and intention was set on not thinking of it, and to aid her resolution, there was the rattle of Dick's latch-key in the front-door, and his voice calling her.

She went out into the little square front hall; there he was, strong and large, and wonderfully undreamlike.

"This heat's a scandal, it's an outrage, it's an abomination of desolation," he cried, vigorously mopping. "What have we done that Providence should place us in this frying-pan? Let us thwart him, Hester! Let us drive out of this inferno and have our dinner at—I'll whisper it so that he shan't overhear—at Hampton Court!"

She laughed: this plan suited her excellently. They would return late, after the distraction of a fresh scene; and dining out at night was both delicious and stupefying.

"The very thing," she said, "and I'm sure Providence didn't hear. Let's start now!"

"Rather. Any letters for me?"

He walked to the table where there were a few rather uninteresting-looking envelopes with half penny stamps.

"Ah, receipted bill," he said. "Just a reminder of one's folly in paying it. Circular ... unasked advice to invest in German marks.... Circular begging letter, beginning 'Dear Sir or Madam.' Such impertinence to ask one to subscribe to something without ascertaining one's sex.... Private view, portraits at the Walton Gallery.... Can't go: business meetings all day. You might like to have a look in, Hester. Some one told me there were some fine Vandycks. That's all: let's be off."

Hester spent a thoroughly reassuring evening, and though she thought of telling Dick about the dream that had so deeply imprinted itself on her consciousness all day, in order to hear the great laugh he would have given her for being such a goose, she refrained from doing so, since nothing that he could say would be so tonic to these fantastic fears as his general robustness. Besides, she would have to account for its disturbing effect, tell him that it was once familiar to her, and recount the sequel of the nightmares that followed. She would neither think of them, nor mention them: it was wiser by far just to soak herself in his extraordinary sanity, and wrap herself in his affection.... They dined out-of-doors at a river-side restaurant and strolled about afterwards, and it was very nearly midnight when, soothed with coolness and fresh air, and the vigour of his strong companionship, she let herself into the house, while he took the car back to the garage. And now she marvelled at the mood which had beset her all day, so distant and unreal had it become. She felt as if she had dreamed of shipwreck, and had awoke to find herself in some secure and sheltered garden where no tempest raged nor waves beat. But was there, ever so remotely, ever so dimly, the noise of far-off breakers somewhere?

He slept in the dressing-room which communicated with her bedroom, the door of which was left open for the sake of air and coolness, and she fell asleep almost as soon as her light was out, and while his was still burning. And immediately she began to dream.

She was standing on the sea-shore; the tide was out, for level sands strewn with stranded jetsam glimmered in a dusk that was deepening into night. Though she had never seen the place it was awfully familiar to her. At the head of the beach there was a steep cliff of sand, and perched on the edge of it was a grey church tower. The sea must have encroached and undermined the body of the church, for tumbled blocks of masonry lay close to her at the bottom of the cliff, and there were gravestones there, while others still in place were silhouetted whitely against the sky. To the right of the church tower there was a wood of stunted trees, combed sideways by the prevalent sea-wind, and she knew that along the top of the cliff a few yards inland there lay a path through fields, with wooden stiles to climb, which led through a tunnel of trees and so out into the churchyard. All this she saw in a glance, and waited, looking at the sand-cliff crowned by the church tower, for the terror that was going to reveal itself. Already she knew what it was, and, as so many times before, she tried to run away. But the catalepsy of nightmare was already on her; frantically she strove to move, but her utmost endeavour could not raise a foot from the sand. Frantically she tried to look away from the sand-cliffs close in front of her, where in a moment now the horror would be manifested....

It came. There formed a pale oval light, the size of a man's face, dimly luminous in front of her and a few inches above the level of her eyes. It outlined itself, short reddish hair grew low on the forehead, below were two grey eyes, set very close together, which steadily and fixedly regarded her. On each side the ears stood noticeably away from the head, and the lines of the jaw met in a short pointed chin. The nose was straight and rather long, below it came a hairless lip, and last of all the mouth took shape and colour, and there lay the crowning terror. One side of it, soft-curved and beautiful, trembled into a smile, the other side, thick and gathered together as by some physical deformity, sneered and lusted.

The whole face, dim at first, gradually focused itself into clear outline: it was pale and rather lean, the face of a young man. And then the lower lip dropped a little, showing the glint of teeth, and there was the sound of speech. "I shall soon come for you now," it said, and on the words it drew a little nearer to her, and the smile broadened. At that the full hot blast of nightmare poured in upon her. Again she tried to run, again she tried to scream, and now she could feel the breath of that terrible mouth upon her. Then with a crash and a rending like the tearing asunder of soul and body she broke the spell, and heard her own voice yelling, and felt with her fingers for the switch of her light. And then she saw that the room was not dark, for Dick's door was open, and the next moment, not yet undressed, he was with her.

"My darling, what is it?" he said. "What's the matter?"

She clung desperately to him, still distraught with terror.

"Ah, he has been here again," she cried. "He says he will soon come to me. Keep him away, Dick."

For one moment her fear infected him, and he found himself glancing round the room.

"But what do you mean?" he said. "No one has been here."

She raised her head from his shoulder.

"No, it was just a dream," she said. "But it was the old dream, and I was terrified. Why, you've not undressed yet. What time is it?"

"You haven't been in bed ten minutes, dear," he said. "You had hardly put out your light when I heard you screaming."

She shuddered.

"Ah, it's awful," she said. "And he will come again...."

He sat down by her.

"Now tell me all about it," he said.

17

She shook her head.

"No, it will never do to talk about it," she said, "it will only make it more real. I suppose the children are all right, are they?"

"Of course they are. I looked in on my way upstairs."

"That's good. But I'm better now, Dick. A dream hasn't anything real about it, has it? It doesn't mean anything?"

He was quite reassuring on this point, and soon she quieted down. Before he went to bed he looked in again on her, and she was asleep.

Hester had a stern interview with herself when Dick had gone down to his office next morning. She told herself that what she was afraid of was nothing more than her own fear. How many times had that ill-omened face come to her in dreams, and what significance had it ever proved to possess? Absolutely none at all, except to make her afraid. She was afraid where no fear was: she was guarded, sheltered, prosperous, and what if a nightmare of childhood returned? It had no more meaning now than it had then, and all those visitations of her childhood had passed away without trace.... And then, despite herself, she began thinking over that vision again. It was grimly identical with all its previous occurrences, except.... And then, with a sudden shrinking of the heart, she remembered that in earlier years those terrible lips had said: "I shall come for you when you are older," and last night they had said: "I shall soon come for you now." She remembered, too, that in the warning dream the sea had encroached, and it had now demolished the body of the church. There was an awful consistency about these two changes in the otherwise identical visions. The years had brought their change to them, for in the one the encroaching sea had brought down the body of the church, in the other the time was now near....

It was no use to scold or reprimand herself, for to bring her mind to the contemplation of the vision meant merely that the grip of terror closed on her again; it was far wiser to occupy herself, and starve her fear out by refusing to bring it the sustenance of thought. So she went about her household duties, she took the children out for their airing in the park, and then, determined to leave no moment unoccupied, set off with the card of invitation to see the pictures in the private view at the Walton Gallery. After that her day was full enough, she was lunching out, and going on to a matinée, and by the time she got home Dick would have returned, and they would drive down to his little house at Rye for the week-end. All Saturday and Sunday she would be playing golf, and she felt that fresh air and physical fatigue would exorcise the dread of these dreaming fantasies.

The gallery was crowded when she got there; there were friends among the sightseers, and the inspection of the pictures was diversified by cheerful conversation. There were two or three fine Raeburns, a couple of Sir Joshuas, but the gems, so she gathered, were three Vandycks that hung in a small room by themselves. Presently she strolled in there, looking at her catalogue. The first of them, she saw, was a portrait of Sir Roger Wyburn. Still chatting to her friend she raised her eye and saw it….

Her heart hammered in her throat, and then seemed to stand still altogether. A qualm, as of some mental sickness of the soul overcame her, for there in front of her was he who would soon come for her. There was the reddish hair, the projecting ears, the greedy eyes set close together, and the mouth smiling on one side, and on the other gathered up into the sneering menace that she knew so well. It might have been her own nightmare rather than a living model which had sat to the painter for that face.

"Ah, what a portrait, and what a brute!" said her companion. "Look, Hester, isn't that marvellous?"

She recovered herself with an effort. To give way to this ever-mastering dread would have been to allow nightmare to invade her waking life, and there, for sure, madness lay. She forced herself to look at it again, but there were the steady and eager eyes regarding her; she could almost fancy the mouth began to move. All round her the crowd bustled and chattered, but to her own sense she was alone there with Roger Wyburn.

And yet, so she reasoned with herself, this picture of him—for it was he and no other—should have reassured her. Roger Wyburn, to have been painted by Vandyck, must have been dead near on two hundred years; how could he be a menace to her? Had she seen that portrait by some chance as a child; had it made some dreadful impression on her, since overscored by other memories, but still alive in the mysterious subconsciousness, which flows eternally, like some dark underground river, beneath the surface of human life? Psychologists taught that these early impressions fester or poison the mind like some hidden abscess. That might account for this dread of one, nameless no longer, who waited for her.

That night down at Rye there came again to her the prefatory dream, followed by the nightmare, and clinging to her husband as the terror began to subside, she told him what she had resolved to keep to herself. Just to tell it brought a measure of comfort, for it was so outrageously fantastic, and his robust common sense upheld her. But when on their return to London there was a recurrence of these visions, he made short work of her demur and took her straight to her doctor.

"Tell him all, darling," he said. "Unless you promise to do that, I will. I can't have you worried like this. It's all nonsense, you know, and doctors are wonderful people for curing nonsense."

She turned to him.

"Dick, you're frightened," she said quietly.

He laughed.

"I'm nothing of the kind," he said, "but I don't like being awakened by your screaming. Not my idea of a peaceful night. Here we are."

The medical report was decisive and peremptory. There was nothing whatever to be alarmed about; in brain and body she was perfectly healthy, but she was run down. These disturbing dreams were, as likely as not, an effect, a symptom of her condition, rather than the cause of it, and Dr. Baring unhesitatingly recommended a complete change to some bracing place. The wise thing would be to send her out of this stuffy furnace to some quiet place to where she had never been. Complete change; quite so. For the same reason her husband had better not go with her; he must pack her off to, let us say, the East coast. Sea-air and coolness and complete idleness. No long walks; no long bathings; a dip, and a deck-chair on the sands. A lazy, soporific life. How about Rushton? He had no doubt that Rushton would set her up again. After a week or so, perhaps, her husband might go down and see her. Plenty of sleep—never mind the nightmares—plenty of fresh air.

Hester, rather to her husband's surprise, fell in with this suggestion at once, and the following evening saw her installed in solitude and tranquillity. The little hotel was still almost empty, for the rush of summer tourists had not yet begun, and all day she sat out on the beach with the sense of a struggle over. She need not fight the terror any more; dimly it seemed to her that its malignancy had been relaxed. Had she in some way yielded to it and done its secret bidding? At any rate no return of its nightly visitations had occurred, and she slept long and dreamlessly, and woke to another day of quiet. Every morning there was a line for her from Dick, with good news of himself and the children, but he and they alike seemed somehow remote, like memories of a very distant time. Something had driven in between her and them, and she saw them as if through glass. But equally did the memory of the face of Roger Wyburn, as seen on the master's canvas or hanging close in front of her against the crumbling sand-cliff, become blurred and indistinct, and no return of her nightly terrors visited her. This truce from all emotion reacted not on her mind alone, lulling her with a sense of soothed security, but on her body also, and she began to weary of this day-long inactivity.

The village lay on the lip of a stretch of land reclaimed from the sea. To the north the level marsh, now beginning to glow with the pale bloom of the sea-lavender, stretched away featureless till it lost itself in distance, but to the south a spur of hill came down to the shore ending in a wooded promontory. Gradually, as her physical health increased, she began to wonder what lay beyond this ridge which cut short the view, and one afternoon she walked across the intervening level and strolled up its wooded slopes. The day was close and windless, the invigorating sea-breeze which till now had spiced the heatwith freshness had died, and she looked forward to finding a current of air stirring when she had topped the hill. To the south a mass of dark cloud lay along the horizon, but there was no imminent threat of storm. The slope was easily surmounted, and presently she stood at the top and found herself on the edge of a tableland of wooded pasture, and following the path, which ran not far from the edge of the cliff, she came out into more open country. Empty fields, where a few sheep were grazing, mounted gradually upwards. Wooden stiles made a communication in the hedges that bounded them. And there, not a mile in front of her, she saw a wood, with trees growing slantingly away from the push of the prevalent sea winds, crowning the upward slope, and over the top of it peered a grey church tower.

For the moment, as the awful and familiar scene identified itself, Hester's heart stood still: the next a wave of courage and resolution poured in upon her. Here, at last was the scene of that prefatory dream, and here was she presented with the opportunity of fathoming and dispelling it. Instantly her mind was made up, and under the strange twilight of the shrouded sky, she walked swiftly on through the fields she had so often traversed in sleep, and up to the wood, beyond which he was waiting for her. She closed her ears against the clanging bell of terror, which now she could silence for ever, and unfalteringly entered that dark tunnel of wood. Soon in front of her the trees began to thin, and through them, now close at hand, she saw the church tower. In a few yards farther she came out of the belt of trees, and round her were the monuments of a graveyard long disused. The cliff was broken off close to the church tower: between it and the edge there was no more of the body of the church than a broken arch, thick hung with ivy. Round this she passed and saw below the ruin of fallen masonry, and the level sands strewn with headstones and disjected rubble, and at the edge of the cliff were graves already cracked and toppling. But there was no one here, none waited for her, and the churchyard where she had so often pictured him was as empty as the fields she had just traversed.

A huge elation filled her; her courage had been rewarded, and all the terrors of the past became to her meaningless phantoms. But there was no time to linger, for now the storm threatened, and on the horizon a blink of lightning was followed by a crackling peal. Just as she turned to go her eye fell on a tombstone that was balanced on the very edge of the cliff, and she read on it that here lay the body of Roger Wyburn.

Fear, the catalepsy of nightmare, rooted her for the moment to the spot; she stared in stricken amazement at the moss-grown letters; almost she expected to see that fell terror of a face rise and hover over his resting-place. Then the fear which had frozen her lent her wings, and with hurrying feet she sped through the arched pathway in the wood and out into the fields. Not one backward glance did she give till she had come to the edge of the ridge above the village, and, turning, saw the pastures she had traversed empty of any living presence. None had followed; but the sheep, apprehensive of the coming storm, had ceased to feed, and were huddling under shelter of the stunted hedges.

Her first idea, in the panic of her mind, was to leave the place at once, but the last train for London had left an hour before, and besides, where was the use of flight if it was the spirit of a man long dead from which she fled? The distance from the place where his bones lay did not afford her safety; that must be sought for within. But she longed for Dick's sheltering and confident presence; he was arriving in any case to-morrow, but there were long dark hours before to-morrow, and who could say what the perils and dangers of the coming night might be? If he started this evening instead of to-morrow morning, he could motor down here in four hours, and would be with her by ten o'clock or eleven. She wrote an urgent telegram: "Come at once," she said. "Don't delay."

The storm which had flickered on the south now came quickly up, and soon after it burst in appalling violence. For preface there were but a few large drops that splashed and dried on the roadway as she came back from the post-office, and just as she reached the hotel again the roar of the approaching rain sounded, and the sluices of heaven were opened. Through the deluge flared the fire of the lightning, the thunder crashed and echoed overhead, and presently the street of the village was a torrent of sandy turbulent water, and sitting there in the dark one picture leapt floating before her eyes, that of the tombstone of Roger Wyburn, already tottering to its fall at the edge of the cliff of the church tower. In such rains as these, acres of the cliffs were loosened; she seemed to hear the whisper of the sliding sand that would precipitate those perished sepulchres and what lay within to the beach below.

By eight o'clock the storm was subsiding, and as she dined she was handed a telegram from Dick, saying that he had already started and sent this off _en route_. By half-past ten, therefore, if all was well, he would be here, and somehow he would stand between her and her fear. Strange how a few days ago both it and the thought of him had become distant and dim to her; now the one was as vivid as the other, and she counted the minutes to his arrival. Soon the rain ceased altogether, and looking out of the curtained window of her sitting-room where she sat watching the slow circle of the hands of the clock, she saw a tawny moon rising over the sea. Before it had climbed to the zenith, before her clock had twice told the hour again, Dick would be with her.

It had just struck ten when there came a knock at her door, and the page-boy entered with the message that a gentleman had come for her. Her heart leaped at the news; she had not expected Dick for half an hour yet, and now the lonely vigil was over. She ran downstairs, and there was the figure standing on the step outside. His face was turned away from her; no doubt he was giving some order to his chauffeur. He was outlined against the white moonlight, and in contrast with that, the gas-jet in the entrance just above his head gave his hair a warm, reddish tinge.

She ran across the hall to him.

"Ah, my darling, you've come," she said. "It was good of you. How quick you've been!" Just as she laid her hand on his shoulder he turned. His arm was thrown out round her, and she looked into a face with eyes close set, and a mouth smiling on one side, the other, thick and gathered together as by some physical deformity, sneered and lusted.

The nightmare was on her; she could neither run nor scream, and supporting her dragging steps, he went forth with her into the night.

Half an hour later Dick arrived. To his amazement he heard that a man had called for his wife not long before, and that she had gone out with him. He seemed to be a stranger here, for the boy who had taken his message to her had never seen him before, and presently surprise began to deepen into alarm; enquiries were made outside the hotel, and it appeared that a witness or two had seen the lady whom they knew to be staying there walking, hatless, along the top of the beach with a man whose arm was linked in hers. Neither of them knew him, but one had seen his face and could describe it.

The direction of the search thus became narrowed down, and though with a lantern to supplement the moonlight they came upon footprints which might have been hers, there were no marks of any who walked beside her. But they followed these until they came to an end, a mile away, in a great landslide of sand, which had fallen from the old churchyard on the cliff, and had brought down with it half the tower and a gravestone, with the body that had lain below.

The gravestone was that of Roger Wyburn, and his body lay by it, untouched by corruption or decay, though two hundred years had elapsed since it was interred there. For a week afterwards the work of searching the landslide went on, assisted by the high tides that gradually washed it away. But no further discovery was made.

III

SPINACH

Ludovic Byron and his sister Sylvia had adopted these pretty, though quite incredible names because those for which their injudicious parents and god-parents were responsible were not so suitable, though quite as incredible. They rightly felt that there was a lack of spiritual suggestiveness in Thomas and Caroline Carrot which would be a decided handicap in their psychical careers, and would cool rather than kindle the faith of those inquirers who were so eager to have séances with the Byrons.

The change, however, had not been made without earnest thought on their parts, for they were two very scrupulous young people, and wondered whether it would be "acting a lie" thus to profess to be what they were not, and whether, in consequence, the clearness of their psychical sight would be dimmed. But they found to their great joy that their spiritual guides or controls, Asteria and Violetta, communicated quite as freely with the Byrons as with the Carrots, and by now they called each other by their assumed names quite naturally, and had almost themselves forgotten that they had ever been other than what they were styled on their neat professional engagement cards.

While it would be tedious to trace Ludovic's progress from the time when it was first revealed to him that he had rare mediumistic gifts down to the present day, when he was quite at the head of his interesting profession, it is necessary to explain the manner in which his powers were manifested. When the circle was assembled (fees payable in advance), he composed himself in his chair, and seemed to sink into a sort of trance, in which Asteria took possession of him and communicated through his mouth with the devotees. Asteria, when living on the material plane, had been a Greek maiden of ancient Athens, who had become a Christian and suffered martyrdom in Rome about the same time as St. Peter. She had wonderful things to tell them all about her experiences on this earth, a little vague, perhaps, as was only natural after so long a lapse of time, but she spoke dreamily yet convincingly about the Parthenon and the Forum and the Ægean sea (so blue) and the catacombs (so black), and the beautiful Italian and Greek sunsets, and this was all the more remarkable because Ludovic had never been outside the country of his birth.

But far more interesting to the circle, any of whom could take a ticket for Rome or Athens and see the sunsets and the catacombs for themselves, were the encouraging things she said about her present existence. Everyone was wonderfully happy and busy helping those who had lately passed over to the other side, and they all lived in an industrious ecstasy of spiritual progress. There were refreshments and relaxations as well, quantities of the most beautiful flowers and exquisite fruits and crystal rivers and azure mountains, and flowing robes and delightful habitations. None of these things was precisely material; you "thought" a flower or a robe, and there it was!

Asteria knew many of the friends and relatives, who had passed over, of Ludovic's circle, and they sent through her loving messages and sweet thoughts. There was George, for instance, did any of the sitters know George? Very often somebody did know George. George was the late husband of one of the sitters, or the father of another, or the little son, who had passed over, of a third, and so George would say how happy he was, and how much love he sent. Then Asteria would tell them that Jane wanted to talk to her dear one, and if nobody knew Jane, it was Mary. And Asteria explained quite satisfactorily how it was that, among all the thousands who were continually passing over, just those who had friends and relations among the ladies and gentlemen who sat with Ludovic Byron were clever enough to "spot" Asteria as being his spiritual guide, who would put them into communication with their loved ones. This was due to currents of sympathy which immediately drew them to her.

Then, when the séance had gone on for some time, Asteria would say that the power was getting weak, and she would bid them good-bye and fade into silence. Presently Ludovic came out of his trance, and they would all tell him how wonderful it had been. At other séances he would not go into trance at all, but Asteria used his hand and his pencil, and wrote pages of automatic script in quaint, slightly foreign English, with here and there a word in strange and undecipherable characters, which was probably Greek. George and Jane and Mary were then dictating to Asteria, who caused Ludovic to write down what she said, and sometimes they were very playful, and did not like their wife's hat or their husband's tie, just by way of showing that they were really there. And then any member of the circle could ask Asteria questions, and she gave them beautiful answers.

Sylvia and her guide, Violetta, were not in so advanced a stage of development as Ludovic and Asteria; indeed, it was only lately that Sylvia had discovered that she had psychical gifts and had got into touch with her guide. Violetta had been a Florentine lady of noble birth, and was born (on the material plane) in the year 1452, which was a very interesting date, as it made her an exact contemporary of Savonarola and Leonardo da Vinci. She had often heard Savonarola preach, and had seen Leonardo at his easel, and it was splendid to know that Savonarola often preached now to enraptured audiences, and that Leonardo was producing pictures vastly superior to anything he had done on earth. They were not material pictures exactly, but thought-pictures. He thought them, and there the pictures were. This corresponded precisely with what Asteria had said about the flowers, and was, therefore, corroborative evidence.

This winter and spring had been a very busy time for Ludovic, and Mrs. Sapson, one of the most regular attendants at his séances, had been trying to persuade him to go for a short holiday. He was very unwilling to do so, for he was giving five full séances every day (which naturally "mounted up,") and he was loth to abandon, even for a short time, the work that so many people found so enlightening. But then Mrs. Sapson had been very clever, and had asked Asteria at one of the séances whether he ought not to take a rest, and Asteria distinctly said: "Wisdom counsels prudence; be it so." After the séance was over, therefore, Mrs. Sapson, strong in spiritual support, renewed her arguments with redoubled force. She was a large, emphatic widow, who received no end of messages from her husband, William. He had been a choleric stockbroker on this plane, but his character had marvellously mellowed and improved, and now he knew what a waste of time it had been to make so much money and lose so much temper.

"Dear Mr. Ludovic," she said, "you must have a rest. You can't fly in the face of sweet Asteria. Besides, I have just got a lovely plan for you. I own a charming little cottage near Rye, which is vacant. My tenant has—has suddenly quitted it. It is a dear little place, everything quite ready for you. No expense at all, except what you eat and drink, and sea-bathing and golf at your door. Such a place for quiet and meditation, and—who knows—some wonderful visitor (not earthly, of course, for there are no bothering neighbours) might come to you there."

Of course, this charming offer made a great difference. Ludovic felt that he could give up his spiritual work for a fortnight with less of a wrench than was possible when he thought that he would have to pay for lodgings. He expressed his gratitude in suitable terms, and promised to consult Sylvia, who at the moment was engaged with Violetta. She leaped at the idea when it was referred to her, and the matter was instantly settled.

The two were chatting together on the eve of their departure.

"Wonderfully kind of Mrs. Sapson," said Ludovic. "But it's odd that she didn't offer us the cottage before. She was wanting me to take a holiday a month ago."

"Perhaps the tenant has only just left," said Sylvia.

"That may be so. Dear me, the country and sea-breezes! How nice. But I don't mean to be idle."

"Golf?" suggested Sylvia. "Isn't it very difficult?"

He walked across to the table and took up a square parcel, which had just been delivered.

"No, not golf," he said. "But I am going to take up spirit photography. It pays very—I mean it's very helpful. So I've bought a camera and some rolls of films, and the developing and fixing solutions. I shall do it all myself. I used to photograph when I was a boy."

"That must have cost a good deal of money," said Sylvia, who had a great gift for economy.

"Ten pounds, but don't look pained; I think it's worth it. Besides, we get our lodging free. And if I have the power of spirit-photography, it will repay us over and over again."

"Explain the process to me," said Sylvia.

"Well, it's very mysterious, but there's no doubt that if a medium who has got the gift takes a photograph, there sometimes appears on the negative what is called an 'extra.' In other words, if I took a photograph of you, there might appear on the film not only your photograph, but that of some spirit, connected with you or the place, standing by you, or perhaps its face floating in the air near you. It would make another branch of our work, it would bring in fresh clients. The old ones too; I think they want something new. Mrs. Sapson would love a photograph of herself with her William leaning over her shoulder. Anyhow, it's worth trying. I shall practise down at the cottage."

He put the parcel containing the photographic apparatus with other property for packing, and made himself comfortable in his chair.

"I want you to work, too," he said. "I want you to develop your _rapport_ with Violetta. There's nothing like practice. Mediumistic power is just as much a gift as music. But you must practice on the piano to be able to play."

The two were alone, and the utmost confidence existed between them. They talked to each other with a frankness which would have appalled their sitters.

"Sometimes I wonder whether I have any mediumistic power at all," she said. "I get in a dreamy sort of state when I am writing automatic script, but is Violetta really communicating, or am I only putting down the thoughts of my sub-conscious self? Or when Asteria speaks through you is she really an independent intelligence, or is she part of your own?"

Ludovic was in a very candid mood.

"I don't know, and I don't care," he said. "But my conscious self certainly can't invent all the things Asteria says, so they come from outside my normal perceptions. And then, after all, Asteria tells things about George and Jane, and so on, concerning their life on earth, which I never knew at all."

"But their relations who are sitting with you know them," said Sylvia. "Isn't it possible that you may get at those facts through telepathy?"

"Yes, but then that's extremely clever of me if I do," said Ludovic. "And it's just as reasonable to say that it's Asteria. Besides, if it's all me, how do you account for it that Asteria sometimes says something which goes against all my intentions and inclinations? For instance, when she said 'Wisdom counsels prudence: be it so,' in answer to Mrs. Sapson's asking if I was not overworked and wanted a holiday, that quite contradicted my own wishes. I didn't want to go for a holiday at all. Therefore it looks as if Asteria was an external intelligence controlling me."

"Sub-consciously you might have known you wanted a holiday," said the ingenious Sylvia.

"That's far-fetched. Better stick to Asteria. Besides, I sincerely believe that sometimes things come to me from outside my consciousness. And I don't know—not always, that's to say—what Asteria has been telling them while I'm in trance. Sometimes it really astonishes me."

He poured out a moderate whisky-and-soda.

"I'm looking forward to a holiday from séances," he said, "now that it's settled, for, frankly, Asteria has been a little thin and feeble lately. And I'm not sure that Mrs. Sapson doesn't think so, too. I think she feels that she's heard about all that Asteria has got to say, and it would never do to lose her as a sitter. That's why I should very much like to find that I can produce spirit photographs. It—it would vary the menu."

They took with them a grim and capable general servant called Gramsby, and arrived next afternoon at Mrs. Sapson's cottage. It was romantically situated near a range of great sand-dunes which ran along the coast, and was only a few minutes' walk from the sea. The place was very remote; a minute village with a shop or two and a cluster of fishermen's huts stood half a mile away, and inland there stretched the empty levels of the Romney marsh away to Rye, which smouldered distantly in the afternoon sunlight. The cottage itself was an enchanting abode, built of timber and rough-cast, with a broad verandah facing south, and a gay little garden in front. Inside, on the ground floor, there were kitchen and dining-room, and a large living-room with access to the verandah. This was well and plainly furnished and had an open fireplace with a wide hearth for a wood fire and an immense chimney. Logs were ready laid there and, indeed, the whole house had the aspect of having been lately tenanted. Upstairs there were sunny bedrooms facing south, which, overlooking the sand-dunes, gave a restful view of the sea beyond; it was impossible to conceive a more tranquil haven for an overworked medium.

They had a hasty cup of tea, and hurried out to enjoy the last hours of daylight in exploration among the sand-dunes and along the beach, and came back soon after sunset. Though the day had been warm, the evening air had a nip in it, and Sylvia gave a little shiver as they stepped in from the verandah to the sitting-room.

"It's rather cold," she said. "I think I'll light the fire."

Ludovic shared her sensations.

"An excellent idea," he said. "And we'll draw the curtains and be cosy. What a charming room! I shall take some interiors to-morrow. Time exposure, I think they told me, for an interior."

Their supper was soon ready, and presently they came back to the sitting-room and laid out a hectic Patience. But they were both strangely absent-minded, neglecting the most glaring opportunities for getting spaces and putting up kings.

"I can't concentrate on it to-night," said Ludovic. "I feel as if someone was trying to attract my attention…. I wonder if Asteria wants to communicate."

Sylvia looked up at him.

"Now it's very odd that you should say that," she observed. "I feel exactly as if Violetta was wanting to come through, and yet it doesn't seem quite like Violetta."

He gave an uneasy glance round the room.

"A curious sensation," he said. "I have the consciousness of some presence here, which isn't quite Asteria. But it may be she. Tiresome of her, if it is, for she ought to know I came down here for a holiday, considering that she recommended it herself. I think I'll get a pencil and paper, and see if she wants to say anything."

He composed himself in a chair, with the stationery for Asteria on his knee.

"Ask her a question or two, Sylvia," he said, "when I go off."

Sylvia waited till her brother's eyelids fluttered and fell.

"Is that you, Asteria?" she asked.

His hand twitched and quivered. Then the pencil scribbled "Certainly not" in large, firm letters, quite unlike Asteria's pretty writing.

Sylvia asked if it was Violetta, but got an emphatic denial.

"Who is it, then?" she said.

And then a very absurd thing happened. The pencil spelt out "Thomas Spinach."

Sylvia was puzzled for a moment. Then the explanation occurred to her, and she laughed.

"Wake up, dear," she said to Ludovic. "It says it is Thomas Spinach. Of course, that's your sub-conscious self trying to remember Carrot."

But Ludovic did not stir, and to her surprise the pencil began writing again.

"I don't know who you are," wrote the unknown control. "But I'm Spinach, young Spinach. And"—there was a long pause—"I want you to help me. I can't remember … I'm very unhappy."

As she followed the words, there suddenly came a very loud rap on the wall just above her, which considerably startled her, for why, if "Spinach" was an attempt on the part of Ludovic's sub-consciousness to write "Carrot," should he announce his presence? She sprang up, and shook Ludovic by the shoulder.

"Wake up," she said. "There's a strange spirit here, and I don't like it. Wake up, Ludovic."

He came drowsily to himself.

"Hullo!" he said. "Anything been happening? was it Asteria?"

His eye fell on the paper.

"What's all this?" he said. "Thomas Spinach? That's only me. My sub-consciousness said it was Asparagus once."

"But look what it has been writing," said Sylvia.

He read it.

"That's queer," he said. "That can't be me. I'm not very unhappy. I don't want my own help. I know who I am."

He jumped up.

"Most interesting," he said. "It looks like a new control. Young Spinach must be powerful, too; he came through the first time he tried. We'll investigate this, Sylvia. It would be fine to get a new control for our séances."

"But not to-night, Ludovic," said she. "I really shouldn't sleep if you went on now. And he's violent. He made the loudest rap I ever heard."

"Did he, indeed?" said Ludovic. "I must have been in deep trance then, for I never heard it. We'll certainly try to snap him with the camera to-morrow."

The morning was bright and sunny, and directly after breakfast Ludovic set to work with his photography. The first three or four films showed nothing but impenetrable blackness, and a consultation of his handbook convinced him that they must have been over-exposed. He corrected this, and after a few errors on the other side, produced a negative which quite clearly showed Sylvia sitting by the long window into the verandah. This, though it revealed no "extra," was an encouraging achievement, and he took half a dozen more exposures with which he hurried away into the small dark cupboard under the stairs, where he had installed his developing and fixing baths. Shortly afterwards Sylvia heard her name called in crowing, exultant tones, and ran to see what had happened.

"Don't open the door," he called, "or you'll spoil it. But I've got a picture of you with a magnificent extra—a face hanging in the air by your shoulder."

"How lovely!" shouted Sylvia. "Do be quick and fix it."

There was no sort of doubt about it. There she sat by the window, and close by her was a strange, inexplicable face. So much could be seen from the negative, and when a print was taken of it, the details were wonderfully clear. It was the face of a young man; his handsome features wore an expression of agonized entreaty.

"Poor boy!" said Sylvia, sympathetically. "So good looking, too, but somehow I don't like him."

Then a brilliant idea struck her.

"Oh, Ludovic!" she said. "Is it young Spinach?"

He snatched the print from her.

"I must fix it," he said, "or it will be ruined. Of course it's young Spinach. Who else could it be, I should like to know? We'll find out more about him this evening. Fancy obtaining that the very first morning!"

They spent the afternoon on the beach, in order to get in an elevated frame of mind by contemplating the beauties of nature, and after a light supper, prepared for a double séance. Two hooks, so to speak, were baited for Spinach, for in one chair sat Sylvia, with pencil and paper, ready to take down his slightest word, and in another Ludovic, similarly equipped. They both let themselves sink into that drowsy and vacant condition which they knew to be favourable to communications from the unseen, but for a long time they neither of them got a bite. Then Ludovic heard the dash and clatter of his sister's pencil, suddenly beginning to write very rapidly, and this aroused in him disturbing feelings of envy and jealousy, for something was coming through to Sylvia and not to him.

This inharmonious emotion quite dissipated the tranquillity which was a _sine qua non_ of the receptive state, and he got up to see what was coming through to her. Probably some mawkish rubbish from Violetta about Savonarola's sermons. But the moment he saw her paper he was thrilled to the marrow.

"Yes, I'm Thomas Spinach," he read, "and I'm very unhappy. I came and stood by you this morning when the man was photographing. I want you to help me. Oh, do help me! It's something I've forgotten, though it is so important. I want you to look everywhere and see if you can't find something very unusual, and tell them. It is somewhere here. It must be, because I put it there, and I hardly like to tell you what it is, because it's terrible...."

The pencil stopped. Ludovic was wildly excited, and his jealousy of Sylvia was almost forgotten. After all, it was he who had taken Spinach's photograph....

Sylvia's hand continued idle so long that Ludovic, in order to stir it into activity again, began to ask questions.

"Have you passed over, Spinach?" he said.

Her hand began to write in a swift and irritated manner. "Of course I have," it scribbled. "Otherwise I should know where it was."

"Used you to live here?" asked Ludovic. "And when did you pass over?"

"Yes, I lived here," came the answer. "I passed over a week ago. Very suddenly. There was a thunderstorm that night, and I had just finished it all, and was in the garden cooling down, when lightning struck me, and when I came to—on this side, you understand—I couldn't remember where it was."

"Where what was?" asked Ludovic. "Do you mean the thing you had finished? What was it you had finished?"

The pencil seemed to give a loud squeak, as if it was a slate pencil.

"Oh, here it is again," it wrote in trembling characters. "I can't go on now. It's terrible. I'm so frightened. Please, please find it."

Just as on the previous evening, there came an appalling rap somewhere on the wall close to him, and, seriously startled, Ludovic sprang up, and shook Sylvia into consciousness. Whoever this spirit was, it was not a good, kind, mild one like Asteria, who, whenever she rapped, did so very softly and pleasantly.

Sylvia yawned and stretched herself.

"Spinach?" she said, drowsily. "Any Spinach?"

"Yes, dear, quantities," said Ludovic.

"And what did he say? Oh, I went off deep then, Ludovic. I don't know what's been happening. Violetta isn't nearly so powerful. Such an odd feeling! Did I write all that?"

"Yes, in answer to some pretty good questions of mine," he said. "It's really wonderful. We're on the track of young Spinach, or, rather, he's on ours."

Sylvia was reading her manuscript.

"'I passed over a week ago,'" she said. "'Very suddenly—there was a thunderstorm that night——' Why, Ludovic, there was! That's quite true. You slept through it, but I didn't, and I remember reading in the paper that it had been very violent in the Rye district. How strange!"

Ludovic clicked his fingers.

"I know what I'll do," he said. "I shall send a telegram to Mrs. Sapson. Give me a piece of paper. She said that wonderful visitors might perhaps come to me here."

Sylvia grasped his thoughts.

"I see!" she cried. "You mean to tell her that her late tenant, young Thomas Spinach, who was killed by lightning last week, has communicated with us.

That will impress her tremendously, if you think she's had enough of Asteria. Indeed, I shouldn't wonder if she lent us this cottage just in order to test us, and see if we really received messages from the other side. What a score!"

She hastily scribbled on a leaf of her writing-block, counting up the words on her fingers. Her economical mind exerted itself to contrive the message in exactly twelve words.

"There!" she read out triumphantly. "Listen! 'Sapson, 29, Brompton Avenue, London. Tenant Spinach killed last week, thunderstorm, communicated.' Just twelve. You needn't sign it, as it will have the Rye postmark."

"My dear," said he, "it's no time for such petty economies. Better spend a few pence more and make it impressive and rather more intelligible. Give me some paper; I asked you before. And we must make it clear that it's not a chance word of local gossip that has inspired it. I shall tell her about the photograph, too."

Before they went to bed, Ludovic composed a more explicit telegram, and in the course of the next morning he received an enthusiastic reply from Mrs. Sapson.

"All quite correct and most wonderful," she wrote. "Delighted you have got into communication. Find out more, and ask him about his uncle. Wire again if fresh revelations occur."

In order to secure themselves from the possibility of interruption, Sylvia gave Gramsby an afternoon out, which she proposed to spend in the excitements of Rye, and as soon as she was gone the mediums prepared for a séance. As Spinach seemed to fancy Sylvia, she composed herself for the trance-condition, with pencil and paper handy, and Ludovic sat by to ask questions. Very soon Sylvia's eyes closed, her head fell forward, and the pencil she held began to tremble violently, like a motor-car ready to start.

"Are you Spinach?" asked Ludovic, observing these signs of possession. Instantly the pencil began to write.

"Yes; have you found it?"

"We don't know what it is," said Ludovic. Then he remembered Mrs. Sapson's telegram. "Has it anything to do with your uncle?" he asked.

There was a long pause. Then the pencil began to move again.

"Please find him," it wrote.

"But how are we to find your uncle?" asked Ludovic. "We don't know where to look or what he's like. Tell us where to look."

The pencil moved in a most agitated fashion.

"I don't know," it wrote. "If I knew I would tell you. But it's somewhere about. I had just put it somewhere, when the lightning came and killed me, and I can't remember. My memory's gone like—like after concussion of the brain."

An uneasy thought struck Ludovic. Why did young Spinach allude to his uncle as "it"?

"Is your uncle dead?" he asked. "Is it his body that you mean by 'it'?"

Sylvia's fingers writhed as if in mortal agony. Then the pencil jerked out, "Yes."

Ludovic, accustomed as he was to spirits, felt an icy shudder run through him. But he waited in silence, for the pencil looked as if it had something more to write. Then, great heavens! it came.

"I will tell you all," it wrote. "I killed him, and I can't remember where I put him."

A spasm of moral indignation seized Ludovic.

"That was very wrong of you," he justly observed. "But we'll try to help you if you will tell us all about it. Come; you're dead. Nobody can hang you."

Shocked as Ludovic was, and extremely uneasy also at the thought of the proximity not only of the spirit of a murderer, but the corpse of young Spinach's uncle, it was only natural that he should feel an overwhelming professional interest in the revelations that appeared to be imminent. It would be a glorious thing for his career to receive from a departed spirit the first-hand account of this undetected crime, and to be able to corroborate it by the discovery of the corpse. Though he had come down here for a holiday, the chance of such a unique piece of work made him feel quite rested already, for it was impossible to conceive a more magnificent advertisement. What a wonderful confirmation it would be also to Mrs. Sapson's wavering faith in his psychical powers. She would publish the news of it far and wide, and the séances would be more popular than ever. Moreover, there was the chance of learning all sorts of fresh information about the conditions that prevailed on the other side, of a far more sensational and exciting quality than the method of the production of thought-flowers and flowing robes and general love and helpfulness.... He waited with the intensest expectation for anything that Spinach might vouchsafe.

At last it began, and now there was no need for further questions, for the pencil streamed across the page. Sheet after sheet of the writing-block was filled, and twice Ludovic had to sharpen Sylvia's pencil, for the point was quite worn down with these remarkable disclosures, and only made illegible scratches on the paper. For half an hour it careered over the sheets; then finally it made a great scrawl, and Sylvia's hand dropped inert. She stretched and yawned, and came to herself.

The next hour was the most absorbing that Ludovic had ever spent in his professional work. Together they read the account of the crime. Alexander Spinach, the uncle, was the most wicked of elderly gentlemen, who made his nephew's life an intolerable burden to him. He had found out that the orphan boy had committed a petty forgery with regard to a cheque which he had signed with his uncle's name, and, holding exposure and arrest over his head, had made him work for him day and night, fishing and farming and doing the work of the house without a penny-piece of wages, while he himself boozed his days away in the chimney-corner.

Long brooding over his wrongs and the misery of his life made young Spinach (very properly, as he still thought) determine to kill the odious old wretch, and he adroitly poisoned his whisky with weed-killer. He went out to his work next morning as usual, leaving the corpse in the locked-up house, and casually mentioned to the folk he came across that his uncle had gone up to London and would probably not be back for some time. When he returned in the evening he hid the body somewhere, meaning to dig a handsome excavation in the garden, and having buried it, plant some useful vegetables above it. But hardly had he made this temporary disposition of the corpse, than he was struck by lightning in the terrific storm that visited the district a week ago, and killed. When he came to himself on the spiritual plane, he could not remember what he had done with the body.

So far the story was ordinary enough, apart from the interest in the manner of its communication, but now came that part of the confession which these ardent young psychicists saw would be a veritable gold mine to them. For on emerging on the other side, young Spinach found himself terrifyingly haunted not by the spirit, but by the body of his uncle. Just as on the material plane, so he explained, murderers are sometimes haunted by the spirit of their victim, so on the spiritual plane, quite logically, they may be haunted by the body of their victim. His uncle's bodily and palpable presence grimly pursued him wherever he went; even as he gathered sweet thought-flowers or thought-fruits, the terrible body appeared. If he woke at night he found it watching by his bed, if he bathed in the crystal rivers it swam beside him, and he had learned that he could never find peace till it was given proper burial. No doubt, he said, Ludovic had heard of the skeletons of murdered folk being walled up in secret chambers, and how their spirits haunted the place till their bones were discovered and interred. The converse was true on the other side, and while murdered corpses lay about unburied in the material world, their bodies haunted the perpetrator of the crime.

It was here that poor young Spinach's difficulty came in. The sudden lightning-stroke had bereft him of all memory of what he was doing just before, and, puzzle as he might, he could not recollect where he had put the corpse.... Then he broke out into passionate entreaties: "Help me, help me, kind mediums," he wrote. "I know it is somewhere about, so search for it and get it buried. He was an awful old man and I can't describe the agony of being haunted by his beastly body. Find it and have it buried, and then I shall be free from its dreadful presence."

They read this unique document together by the fading light, strung up to the highest pitch of professional interest, and yet peering awfully round from time to time in vague apprehension of what might happen next. During the séance the wind had got up, and now it was moaning round the corners of the house, and dusk was falling rapidly, with prospects of a wild night to follow. The curtains bulged and bellied in the draught, hollow voices sounded in the chimney, and Sylvia clung to her brother.

"I don't like it," she wailed. "I don't like this spirit of Spinach; Violetta and Asteria are far preferable. And then there's 'It.' It is somewhere about, and it may be anywhere."

Ludovic made an attempt at gaiety.

"It may be anywhere, as you say," he remarked, "but it actually is somewhere. And we've got to find it, dear. Better find it before it gets dark. And think of the sensation there will be when we publish the account of how, in answer to the entreaty of a remorseful spirit——"

"But he isn't remorseful," said Sylvia. "There's not a word of remorse, but only terror at being haunted. There's not only a corpse about, but the spirit of an unrepentant murderer. It isn't pleasant. I would sooner be in expensive lodgings than here."

"Oh, nonsense," said Ludovic. "Besides, young Spinach is friendly enough to us. We're his one hope. And if we find it, he will certainly be very grateful. I shouldn't wonder if he sent us many more revelations. Even as it is, how deeply interesting. Nobody ever guessed that there were material ghosts in the spiritual world. But now we must get busy and search for Alexander. Fix your mind on what a tremendously paying experience this will be. Now, where shall we begin? There's the house and the garden——"

"Oh, I hope it will be in the garden," said Sylvia. "But there's no chance of that, for he meant to bury it in the garden afterwards."

"True. We'll begin with the house, then. Now most murderers bury the body under the floor of the kitchen, cover it with quicklime, and fill in with cement."

"But he wouldn't have had time for that," said Sylvia. "Besides, this was to be only a temporary resting-place."

"Perhaps he cut it up," said Ludovic, "and we shall find a piece here and a piece there."

The search began. In the growing dusk, with the wild wind increasing to a gale, they annealed themselves for the gruesome business. They investigated the coal cellar, they peered into housemaids' cupboards, and with quaking hearts examined the woodshed. Here there were signs that its contents had been disturbed, and the sight of an old boot peeping out from behind some logs nearly caused Sylvia to collapse. Then Ludovic got a ladder, and, climbing up to the roof, interrogated the water-tank, from the contents of which they had already drunk. But all their explorations were in vain; there was no sign of the corpse. For a nerve-racking hour they persevered, and a dismal idea occurred to Ludovic.

"It can't be a practical joke on the part of Spinach, can it?" he said "That would be in the worst possible taste. Good gracious, what's that?"

There came a loud tapping at the front door, and Sylvia hid her face on his shoulder.

"That's Spinach," she whispered. "That terrible Spinach!"

They tottered to the door and opened it. On the threshold was a man, who told them he was the carrier from Rye, and brought a note for Miss Byron.

"I'm going back in half an hour, miss," he said, "if there's any answer. A box, I understood."

The note was from Gramsby, who, though unwilling to "upset" them, declined to come back to the cottage. She had heard things, and she didn't like it, and she would be obliged if they would pack her box and send it in.

"The coward!" said Sylvia, trembling violently. "She shan't have her box unless she comes to fetch it."

They went back into the sitting-room, lit the fire, and made it as cheerful as they could with many candles. Their flames wagged ominously in the eddying draughts, and the two drew their chairs close to the hearth. By now the full fury of the gale was unloosed, the whole house shuddered at the blasts, doors creaked, curtains whispered, flurries of rain were flung against the windows, and strange noises and stirrings muttered in the chimney.

"I shall just get warm," said Ludovic, "and then go on with the search. I shan't know a moment's peace till I find it."

"I shan't know a moment's peace when you do!" wailed Sylvia.

They were sitting in the fire almost, and suddenly something up the chimney caught Ludovic's eye.

"What's that?" he said.   ·

He got a candle and held it up the chimney.

"It's a rope," he said, "tied round a staple in the wall."

His look met hers, and read the answering horror there.

"I'm going to undo it," he said. "Step back, Sylvia."

There was no need to say that, for she had already retreated to the farthest corner of the room. He pulled the rope off the staple and let it go.

There was a scrambling, shuffling noise from high up in the chimney, and in a cloud of soot It fell, with a heavy thud, sprawling across the hearth.

They fled into the night; the carrier had only just got to the garden gate.

"Take us into Rye," cried Ludovic. "Take us to the police-station. Murder has been done——"

The account of these amazing events duly appeared in all the psychical papers and many others. Long queues of would-be sitters formed up for the Byron séances, in the hopes of getting fresh revelations from young Spinach. But from association with Asteria and Violetta he gradually became quite commonplace, and only told them about thought-flowers and white robes.

IV

BAGNELL TERRACE

I had been for ten years an inhabitant of Bagnell Terrace, and, like all those who have been so fortunate as to secure a footing there, was convinced that for amenity, convenience, and tranquillity it is unrivalled in the length and breadth of London. The houses are small; we could, none of us, give an evening party or a dance, but we who live in Bagnell Terrace do not desire to do anything of the kind. We do not go in for sounds of revelry at night, nor, indeed, is there much revelry during the day, for we have gone to Bagnell Terrace in order to be anchored in a quiet little backwater. There is no traffic through it, for the terrace is a cul-de-sac, closed at the far end by a high brick wall, along which, on summer nights, cats trip lightly on visits to their friends. Even the cats of Bagnell Terrace have caught something of its discretion and tranquillity, for they do not hail each other with long-drawn yells of mortal agony like their cousins in less well-conducted places, but sit and have quiet little parties like the owners of the houses in which they condescend to be lodged and boarded.

But, though I was more content to be in Bagnell Terrace than anywhere else, I had not got, and was beginning to be afraid I never should get, the particular house which I coveted above all others. This was at the top end of the terrace adjoining the wall that closed it, and in one respect it was unlike the other houses, which so much resemble each other. The others have little square gardens in front of them, where we have our bulbs abloom in the spring, when they present a very gay appearance, but the gardens are too small, and London too sunless to allow of any very effective horticulture. The house, however, to which I had so long turned envious eyes, had no garden in front of it; instead, the space had been used for the erection of a big, square room (for a small garden will make a very well-sized room) connected with the house by a covered passage. Rooms in Bagnell Terrace, though sunny and cheerful, are not large, and just one big room, so it occurred to me, would give the final touch of perfection to those delightful little residences.

Now, the inhabitants of this desirable abode were something of a mystery to our neighbourly little circle, though we knew that a man lived there (for he was occasionally seen leaving or entering his house), he was personally unknown to us. A curious point was that though we had all (though rarely) encountered him on the pavements, there was a considerable discrepancy in the impression he had made on us. He certainly walked briskly, as if the vigour of life was still his, but while I believed that he was a young man, Hugh Abbot, who lived in the house next his, was convinced that, in spite of his briskness, he was not only old, but very old. Hugh and I, life-long bachelor friends, often discussed him in the ramble of conversation when he had dropped in for an after-dinner pipe, or I had gone across for a game of chess. His name was not known to us, so, by reason of my desire for his house, we called him Naboth. We both agreed that there was something odd about him, something baffling and elusive.

I had been away for a couple of months one winter in Egypt; the night after my return Hugh dined with me, and after dinner I produced those trophies which the strongest-minded are unable to refrain from purchasing, when they are offered by an engaging burnoused ruffian in the Valley of the Tombs of the Kings. There were some beads (not quite so blue as they had appeared there), a scarab or two, and for the last I kept the piece of which I was really proud, namely, a small lapis-lazuli statuette, a few inches high, of a cat. It sat square and stiff on its haunches, with upright forelegs, and, in spite of the small scale, so good were the proportions and so accurate the observation of the artist, that it gave the impression of being much bigger. As it stood on Hugh's palm, it was certainly small, but if, without the sight of it, I pictured it to myself, it represented itself as far larger than it really was.

"And the odd thing is," I said, "that though it is far and away the best thing I picked up, I cannot for the life of me remember where I bought it. Somehow I feel that I've always had it."

He had been looking very intently at it. Then he jumped up from his chair and put it down on the chimney-piece.

"I don't think I quite like it," he said, "and I can't tell you why. Oh, a jolly bit of workmanship: I don't mean that. And you can't remember where you got it, did you say? That's odd…. Well, what about a game of chess."

We played a couple of games, without much concentration or fervour, and more than once I saw him glance with a puzzled look at my little image on the chimney-piece. But he said nothing more about it, and when our games were over, he gave me the discursive news of the terrace. A house had fallen vacant and been instantly snapped up.

"Not Naboth's?" I asked.

"No, not Naboth's. Naboth is in possession still. Very much in possession; going strong."

"Anything new?" I asked.

"Oh, just bits of things. I've seen him a good many times lately, and yet I can't get any clear idea of him. I met him three days ago, as I was coming out of my gate, and had a good look at him, and for a moment I agreed with you and thought he was a young man. Then he turned and stared me in the face for a second, and I thought I had never seen anyone so old. Frightfully alive, but more than old, antique, primeval."

"And then?" I asked.

"He passed on, and I found myself, as has so often happened before, quite unable to remember what his face was like. Was he old or young? I didn't know. What was his mouth like, or his nose? But it was the question of his age which was the most baffling."

38

Hugh stretched his feet out towards the blaze, and sank back in his chair, with one more frowning look at my lapis lazuli cat.

"Though after all, what is age?" he said. "We measure age by time, we say 'so many years,' and forget that we're in eternity here and now, just as we say we're in a room or in Bagnell Terrace, though we're much more truly in infinity."

"What has that got to do with Naboth?" I asked.

Hugh beat his pipe out against the bars of the grate before he answered.

"Well, it will probably sound quite cracked to you," he said, "unless Egypt, the land of ancient mystery, has softened your rind of materialism, but it struck me then that Naboth belonged to eternity much more obviously than we do. We belong to it, of course, we can't help that, but he's less involved in this error or illusion of time than we are. Dear me, it sounds amazing nonsense when I put it into words."

I laughed.

"I'm afraid my rind of materialism isn't soft enough yet," I said. "What you say implies that you think Naboth is a sort of apparition, a ghost, a spirit of the dead that manifests itself as a human being, though it isn't one!"

He drew his legs up to him again.

"Yes; it must be nonsense," he said. "Besides he has been so much in evidence lately, and we can't all be seeing a ghost. It doesn't happen. And there have been noises coming from his house, loud and cheerful noises which I've never heard before. Somebody plays an instrument like a flute in that big, square room you envy so much, and somebody beats an accompaniment as if with drums. Odd sort of music; it goes on often now at night.... Well, it's time to go to bed."

Again he glanced up at the chimney-piece.

"Why, it's quite a little cat," he said.

This rather interested me, for I had said nothing to him about the impression left on my mind that it was bigger than its actual dimensions.

"Just the same size as ever," I said.

"Naturally. But I had been thinking of it as life-size for some reason," said he.

I went with him to the door, and strolled out with him into the darkness of an overcast night. As we neared his house, I saw that big patches of light shone into the road from the windows of the square room next door. Suddenly Hugh laid his hand on my arm.

"There!" he said. "The flutes and drums are at it to-night."

The night was very still, but, listen as I would, I could hear nothing but the rumble of traffic in the street beyond the terrace.

"I can't hear it," I said.

Even as I spoke, I heard it, and the wailing noise whisked me back to Egypt again. The boom of the traffic became for me the beat of the drum, and upon it floated just that squeal and wail of the little reed pipes which accompany the Arab dances, tuneless and rhythmless, and as old as the temples of the Nile.

"It's like the Arab music that you hear in Egypt," I said.

As we stood listening it ceased to his ears as well as mine, as suddenly as it had begun, and simultaneously the lights in the windows of the square room were extinguished.

We waited a moment in the roadway opposite Hugh's house, but from next door came no sound at all, nor glimmer of illumination from any of its windows....

I turned; it was rather chilly to one lately arrived from the South.

"Good night," I said, "we'll meet to-morrow sometime."

I went straight to bed, slept at once, and woke with the impress of a very vivid dream on my mind. There was music in it, familiar Arab music, and there was an immense cat somewhere. Even as I tried to recall it, it faded, and I had but time to recognise it as a hash-up of the happenings of the evening before I went to sleep again.

The normal habits of life quickly reasserted themselves. I had work to do, and there were friends to see; all the minute events of each day stitched themselves into the tapestry of life. But somehow a new thread began to be woven into it, though at the time I did not recognise it as such. It seemed trivial and extraneous that I should so often hear a few staves of that odd music from Naboth's house, or that as often as it fixed my attention it was silent again, as if I had imagined, rather than actually heard it. It was trivial, too, that I should so often see Naboth entering or leaving his house. And then one day I had a sight of him, which was unlike any previous experience of mine.

I was standing one morning in the window of my front room. I had idly picked up my lapis lazuli cat, and was holding it in the splash of sunlight that poured in, admiring the soft texture of its surface which, though it was of hard stone, somehow suggested fur. Then, quite casually, I looked up, and there a few yards in front of me, leaning on the railings of my garden, and intently observing not me, but what I held, was Naboth. His eyes, fixed on it, blinked in the April sunshine with some purring sensuous content, and Hugh was right on the question of his age; he was neither old nor young, but timeless.

The moment of perception passed; it flashed on and off my mind like the revolving beam of some distant lighthouse. It was just a ray of illumination, and was instantly shut off again, so that it appeared to my conscious mind like some hallucination. He suddenly seemed aware of me, and turning, walked briskly off down the pavement.

I remember being rather startled, but the effect soon faded, and the incident became to me one of those trivial little things that make a momentary impression and vanish. It was odd, too, but in no way remarkable, that more than once I saw one of those discreet cats of which I

40

have spoken sitting on the little balcony outside my front room, and gravely regarding the interior. I am devoted to cats, and several times I got up in order to open the window and invite it to enter, but each time on my movement it jumped down and slunk away. And April passed into May.

I came back after dining out one night in this month; and found a telephone message from Hugh that I should ring him up on my return. A rather excited voice answered me.

"I thought you would like to know at once," he said. "An hour ago a board was put up on Naboth's house to say that the freehold was for sale. Martin and Smith are the agents. Good night; I'm in bed already."

"You're a true friend," I said.

Early next morning, of course, I presented myself at the house-agent's. The price asked was very moderate, the title perfectly satisfactory. He could give me the keys at once, for the house was empty, and he promised that I could have a couple of days to make up my mind, during which time I was to have the prior right of purchase if I was disposed to pay the full price asked. If, however, I only made an offer, he could not guarantee that the trustees would accept it.... Hot-foot, with the keys in my pocket, I sped back up the terrace again.

I found the house completely empty, not of inhabitants only, but of all else. There was not a blind, not a strip of drugget, not a curtain-rod in it from garret to cellar. So much the better, thought I, for there would be no tenants' fixtures to take on. Nor was there any débris of removal, of straw and waste paper; the house looked as if it was prepared for an occupant instead of just rid of one. All was in apple-pie order, the windows clean, the floors swept, the paint and woodwork bright; it was a clean and polished shell ready for its occupier. My first inspection, of course, was of the big built-out room, which was its chief attraction, and my heart leaped at the sight of its plain spaciousness. On one side was an open fireplace, on the other a coil of pipes for central heating, and at the end, between the windows, a niche let into the wall, as if a statue had once stood there; it might have been designed expressly for my bronze Perseus. The rest of the house presented no particular features; it was on the same plan as my own, and my builder, who inspected it that afternoon, pronounced it to be in excellent condition.

"It looks as if it had been newly done up, and never lived in," he said, "and at the price you mention is a decided bargain."

The same thing struck Hugh when, on his return from his office, I dragged him over to see it.

"Why, it all looks new," he said, "and yet we know that Naboth has been here for years, and was certainly here a week ago. And then there's another thing. When did he remove his furniture? There have been no vans at the house that I have seen."

I was much too pleased at getting my heart's desire to consider anything except that I had got it.

"Oh, I can't bother about little things like that," I said. "Look at my beautiful big room. Piano there, bookcases all along the wall, sofa in front of the fire, Perseus in the niche. Why, it was made for me."

Within the specified two days the house was mine, and within a month papering and distempering, electric fittings, and blinds and curtain rods were finished, and my move began. Two days were sufficient for the transport of my goods, and at the close of the second my old house was dismantled, except for my bedroom, the contents of which would be moved next day. My servants were installed in the new abode, and that night, after a hurried dinner with Hugh, I went back for a couple more hours' work of hauling and tugging and arranging books in the large room, which it was my purpose to finish first. It was a chilly night for May, and I had had a log-fire lit on the hearth, which from time to time I replenished, in intervals of dusting and arranging. Eventually, when the two hours had lengthened themselves into three, I determined to give over for the present, and, much tired, sat down for a recuperative pause on the edge of my sofa and contemplated with satisfaction the result of my labours. At that moment I was conscious that there was a stale, but aromatic, smell in the room that reminded me of the curious odour that hangs about an Egyptian temple. But I put it down to the dust from my books and the smouldering logs.

The move was completed next day, and after another week I was installed as firmly as if I had been there for years. May slipped by, and June, and my new house never ceased to give me a vivid pleasure: it was always a treat to return to it. Then came a certain afternoon when a strange thing happened.

The day had been wet, but towards evening it cleared up: the pavements soon dried, but the road remained moist and miry. I was close to my house on my way home, when I saw form itself on the paving-stones a few yards in front of me the mark of a wet shoe, as if someone invisible to the eye had just stepped off the road. Another and yet another briskly imprinted themselves going up towards my house. For the moment I stood stock still, and then, with a thumping heart I followed. The marks of these strange footsteps preceded me right up to my door: there was one on the very threshold faintly visible.

I let myself in, closing the door, I confess, very quickly behind me. As I stood there I heard a resounding crash from my room, which, so to speak, startled my fright from me, and I ran down the little passage, and burst in. There, at the far end of the room was my bronze Perseus fallen from its niche and lying on the floor. And I knew, by what sixth sense I cannot tell, that I was not alone in the room and that the presence there was no human presence.

Now fear is a very odd thing: unless it is overmastering and overwhelming, it always produces its own reaction. Whatever courage we have rises to meet it, and with courage comes anger that we have given entrance to this unnerving intruder. That, at any rate, was my case now, and I made an effective emotional resistance. My servant came running in to see what the noise was, and we set Perseus on his feet again and examined into the cause of his fall. It was clear enough: a big piece of plaster had broken away from the niche, and that must be repaired and strengthened before we reinstated him. Simultaneously my fear and the sense of an unaccountable presence in the room slipped from me. The footsteps outside were still unexplained and I told myself that if I was to shudder at everything I did not understand, there would be an end to tranquil existence for ever.

I was dining with Hugh that night: he had been away for the last week, only returning to-day, and he had come in before these slightly agitating events happened to announce his arrival and suggest dinner. I noticed that as he stood chatting for a few minutes, he had once or twice sniffed the air but he had made no comment, nor had I asked him if he perceived the strange faint odour that every now and then manifested itself to me. I knew it was a great relief to some secretly-quaking piece of my mind that he was back, for I was convinced that there was some psychic disturbance going on, either subjectively in my mind, or a real invasion from without. In either case his presence was comforting, not because he is of that stalwart breed which believes in nothing beyond the material facts of life, and pooh-poohs these mysterious forces which surround and so strangely interpenetrate existence, but because, while thoroughly believing in them, he has the firm confidence that the deadly and evil powers which occasionally break through into the seeming security of existence are not really to be feared, since they are held in check by forces stronger yet, ready to assist all who realise their protective care. Whether I meant to tell him what had occurred to-day I had not fully determined.

It was not till after dinner that such subjects came up at all, but I had seen there was something on his mind of which he had not spoken yet.

"And your new house," he said at length, "does it still remain as all your fancy painted?"

"I wonder why you ask that," I said.

He gave me a quick glance.

"Mayn't I take any interest in your well-being?" he said.

I knew that something was coming, if I chose to let it.

"I don't think you've ever liked my house from the first," I said. "I believe you think there's something queer about it. I allow that the manner in which I found it empty was odd."

"It was rather," he said. "But so long as it remains empty, except for what you've put in it, it is all right."

I wanted now to press him further.

"What was it you smelt this afternoon in the big room?" I said. "I saw you nosing and sniffing. I have smelt something, too. Let's see if we smelt the same thing."

"An odd smell," he said. "Something dusty and stale, but aromatic."

"And what else have you noticed?" I asked.

He paused a moment.

"I think I'll tell you," he said. "This evening from my window I saw you coming up the pavement, and simultaneously I saw, or thought I saw, Naboth cross the road and walk on in front of you. I wondered if you saw him, too, for you paused as he stepped on to the pavement in front of you, and then you followed him."

I felt my hands grow suddenly cold, as if the warm current of my blood had been chilled.

"No, I didn't see him," I said, "but I saw his step."

"What do you mean?"

"Just what I say. I saw footprints in front of me, which continued on to my threshold."

"And then?"

"I went in, and a terrific crash startled me. My bronze Perseus had fallen from his niche. And there was something in the room."

There was a scratching noise at the window. Without answering, Hugh jumped up and drew aside the curtain. On the sill was seated a large grey cat, blinking in the light. He advanced to the window, and on his approach the cat jumped down into the garden. The light shone out into the road, and we both saw, standing on the pavement just outside, the figure of a man. He turned and looked at me, and then moved away towards my house, next door.

"It's he," said Hugh.

He opened the window and leaned out to see what had become of him. There was no sign of him anywhere, but I saw that light shone from behind the blinds of my room.

"Come on," I said. "Let's see what is happening. Why is my room lit?"

I opened the door of my house with my latch-key, and followed by Hugh went down the short passage to the room. It was perfectly dark, and when I turned the switch, we saw that it was empty. I rang the bell, but no answer came, for it was already late, and doubtless my servants had gone to bed.

"But I saw a strong light from the windows two minutes ago," I said, "and there has been no one here since."

Hugh was standing by me in the middle of the room. Suddenly he threw out his arm as if striking at something. That thoroughly alarmed me.

"What's the matter?" I asked. "What are you hitting at?"

He shook his head.

"I don't know," he said. "I thought I saw——But I'm not sure. But we're in for something if we stop here. Something is coming, though I don't know what."

The light seemed to me to be burning dim; shadows began to collect in the corner of the room, and though outside the night had been clear, the air here was growing thick with a foggy vapour, which smelt dusty and stale and aromatic. Faintly, but getting louder as we waited there in silence, I heard the throb of drums and the wail of flutes. As yet I had no feeling that there were other presences in the place beyond ours, but in the growing dimness I knew that something was coming nearer. Just in front of me was the empty niche from which my bronze had fallen, and looking at it, I saw that something was astir. The shadow within it began to shape itself into a form, and out of it there gleamed two points of greenish light. A moment more and I saw that they were eyes of antique and infinite malignity.

I heard Hugh's voice in a sort of hoarse whisper.

"Look there!" he said. "It's coming! Oh, my God, it's coming!"

Sudden as the lightning that leaps from the heart of the night it came. But it came not with blaze and flash of light, but, as it were, with a stroke of blinding darkness, that fell not on the eye, or on any material sense, but on the spirit, so that I cowered under it in some abandonment of terror. It came from those eyes which gleamed in the niche, and which now I saw to be set in the face of the figure that stood there. The form of it, naked, but for a loin-cloth, was that of a man, the head seemed now human, now to be that of some monstrous cat. And as I looked, I knew that if I continued looking there I should be submerged and drowned in that flood of evil that poured from it. As in some catalepsy of nightmare I struggled to tear my eyes from it, but still they were riveted there, gazing on incarnate hate.

Again I heard Hugh's whisper.

"Defy it," he said. "Don't yield an inch."

A swarm of disordered and hellish images were buzzing in my brain, and now I knew as surely as if actual words had been spoken to us that the presence there told me to come to it.

"I've got to go to it," I said. "It's making me go."

I felt his hand tighten on my arm.

"Not a step," he said. "I'm stronger than it is. It will know that soon. Just pray—pray."

Suddenly his arm shot out in front of me, pointing at the presence.

"By the power of God," he shouted. "By the power of God."

There was dead silence. The light of those eyes faded, and then came dawn on the darkness of the room. It was quiet and orderly, the niche was empty, and there on the sofa by me was Hugh, his face white and streaming with sweat.

"It's over," he said, and without pause fell fast asleep.

Now we have often talked over together what happened that evening. Of what seemed to happen, I have already given the account, which anyone may believe or not, precisely as they please. He, as I, was conscious of a presence wholly evil, and he tells me that all the time that those eyes gleamed from the niche, he was trying to realise what he believed, namely, that only one power in the world is Omnipotent, and that the moment he gained that realisation the presence collapsed. What exactly that presence was it is impossible to say. It looks as if it was the essence or spirit of one of those mysterious Egyptian cults, of which the force survived, and was seen and felt in this quiet terrace. That it was embodied in Naboth seems (among all these incredibilities) possible, and Naboth certainly has never been seen again. Whether or not it was connected with the worship and cult of cats might occur to the mythological mind, and it is perhaps worthy of record that I found next morning my little lapis lazuli image, which stood on the chimneypiece, broken into fragments. It was too badly damaged to mend, and I am not sure that, in any case, I should have attempted to have it restored.

Finally, there is no more tranquil and pleasant room in London than the one built out in front of my house in Bagnell Terrace.

V

A TALE OF AN EMPTY HOUSE

It had been a disastrous afternoon: rain had streamed incessantly from a low grey sky, and the road was of the vilest description. There were sections consisting of sharp flints, newly laid down and not yet rolled into amenity, and the stretches in between were worn into deep ruts and bouncing holes, so that it was impossible anywhere to travel at even a moderate speed. Twice we had punctured, and now, as the stormy dusk began to fall, something went wrong with the engine, and after crawling on for a hundred yards or so we stopped. My driver, after a short investigation, told me that there was a half-hour's tinkering to be done, and after that we might, with luck, trundle along in a leisurely manner, and hope eventually to arrive at Crowthorpe which was the proposed destination.

We had come, when this stoppage occurred, to a crossroad. Through the driving rain I could see on the right a great church, and in front a huddle of houses. A consultation of the map seemed to indicate that this was the village of Riddington. The guide-book added the information that Riddington possessed an hotel, and the sign-post at the corner endorsed them both. To the right along the main road, into which we had just struck, was Crowthorpe, fifteen miles away and straight in front of us, half a mile distant, was the hotel.

The decision was not difficult. There was no reason why I should get to Crowthorpe to-night instead of to-morrow, for the friend whom I was to meet there would not arrive until next afternoon and it was surely better to limp half a mile with a spasmodic engine than to attempt fifteen on this inclement evening.

"We'll spend the night here," I said to my chauffeur. "The road dips down hill, and it's only half a mile to the hotel. I daresay we shall get there without using the engine at all. Let's try, anyhow."

We hooted and crossed the main road, and began to slide very slowly down a narrow street. It was impossible to see much, but on either side there were little houses with lights gleaming through blinds, or with blinds still undrawn, revealing cosy interiors. Then the incline grew steeper, and close in front of us I saw masts against a sheet of water that appeared to stretch unbroken into the rain-shrouded gloom of the gathering night.

Riddington then must be on the open sea, though how it came about that boats should be tied up to an open quay-wall was a puzzle, but perhaps there was some jetty, invisible in the darkness, which protected them. I heard the chauffeur switch on his engine, as we made a sharp turn to the left, and we passed below a long row of lighted windows, shining out on to a rather narrow road, on the right edge of which the water lapped. Again he turned sharply to the left, described a half-circle on crunching gravel, and drew up at the door of the hotel. There was a room for me, there was a garage, there was a room for him, and dinner had not long begun.

Among the little excitements and surprises of travel there is none more delightful than that of waking in a new place at which one has arrived after nightfall on the previous evening. The mind has received a few hints and dusky impressions, and probably during sleep it has juggled with these, constructing them into some sort of coherent whole and next morning its anticipations are put to the proof. Usually the eye has seen more than it has consciously registered, and the brain has fitted together as in the manner of a jig-saw puzzle a very fair presentment of its immediate surroundings. When I woke next morning a brilliantly sunny sky looked in at my windows; there was no sound of wind or of breaking waves, and before getting up and verifying my impressions of the night before I lay and washed-in my imagined picture. In front of my windows there would be a narrow roadway bordered by a quay-wall: there would be a breakwater, forming a harbour for the boats that lay at anchor there, and away, away to the horizon would stretch an expanse of still and glittering sea. I ran over these points in my mind; they seemed an inevitable inference from the glimpses of the night before and then, assured of my correctness, I got out of bed and went to the window.

I have never experienced so complete a surprise. There was no harbour, there was no breakwater, and there was no sea. A very narrow channel, three-quarters choked with sand-banks on which now rested the boats whose masts I had seen the previous evening, ran parallel to the road, and then turned at right angles and went off into the distance. Otherwise no water of any sort was visible; right and left and in front stretched a limitless expanse of shining grasses with tufts of shrubby growth, and great patches of purple sea-lavender. Beyond were tawny sand-banks, and further yet a line of shingle and scrub and sand-dunes. But the sea which I had expected to fill the whole circle of the visible world till it met the sky on the horizon, had totally disappeared.

After the first surprise at this colossal conjuring trick was over, I dressed quickly, in order to ascertain from local authorities how it was done. Unless some hallucination had poisoned my perceptive faculties, there must be an explanation of this total disappearance, alternately, of sea and land, and the key, when supplied, was simple enough. That line of shingle and scrub and sand dunes on the horizon was a peninsula running for four or five miles parallel with the land, forming the true beach, and it enclosed this vast basin of sand-banks and mud-banks and level lavender-covered marsh, which was submerged at high tide, and made an estuary. At low tide it was altogether empty but for the stream that struggled out through various channels to the mouth of it two miles away to the left, and there was easy passage across it for a man who carried his shoes and stockings, to the far sand dunes and beaches which terminated at Riddington Point, while at high tide you could sail out from the quay just in front of the hotel and be landed there.

The tide would be out of the estuary for five or six hours yet; I could spend the morning on the beach, or, taking my lunch, walk out to the Point, and be back before the returning waters rendered the channel impassable. There was good bathing on the beach, and there was a colony of terns who nested there.

Already, as I ate my breakfast at a table in the window overlooking the marsh, the spell and attraction of it had begun to work. It was so immense and so empty; it had the allure of the desert about it, with none of the desert's intolerable monotony, for companies of chiding gulls hovered over it, and I could hear the pipe of redshank and the babble of curlews. I was due to meet Jack Granger in Crowthorpe that evening, but if I went I knew that I should persuade him to come back to Riddington, and from my knowledge of him, I was aware that he would feel the spell of the place not less potent than I. So, having ascertained that there was a room for him here, I wrote him a note saying that I had found the most amazing place in the world, and told my chauffeur to take the car into Crowthorpe to meet the train that afternoon and bring him here. And with a perfectly clear conscience, I set off with a towel and a packet of lunch in my pocket to explore vaguely and goallessly that beckoning immensity of lavender-covered, bird-haunted expanse.

My way, as pointed out to me, led first along a sea-bank which defended the drained pastureland on the right of it from the high tides, and at the corner of that I struck into the basin of the estuary. A contour line of jetsam, withered grass, strands of seaweed, and the bleached shells of little crabs showed where the last tide had reached its height, and inside it the marsh growth was still wet. Then came a stretch of mud and pebbles, and presently I was wading through the stream that flowed down to the sea. Beyond that were banks of ribbed sand swept by the incoming tides, and soon I regained the wide green marshes on the further side, beyond which was the bar of shingle that fringed the sea.

I paused as I re-shod myself. There was not a sign of any living human being within sight, but never have I found myself in so exhilarating a solitude. Right and left were spread the lawns of sea-lavender, starred with pink tufts of thrift and thickets of suæda bushes. Here and there were pools left in depressions of the ground by the retreated tide, and here were patches of smooth black mud, out of which grew, like little spikes of milky-green asparagus, a crop of glass-wort, and all these happy vegetables flourished in sunshine or rain or the salt of the flooding tides with impartial amphibiousness. Overhead was the immense arc of the sky, across which flew now a flight of duck, hurrying with necks outstretched, and now a lonely black-backed gull, flapping his ponderous way seawards. Curlews were bubbling, and redshank and ringed plover fluting, and now as I trudged up the shingle bank, at the bottom of which the marsh came to an end, the sea, blue and waveless, lay stretched and sleeping, bordered by a strip of sand, on which far off a mirage hovered. But from end to end of it, as far as eye could see, there was no sign of human presence.

I bathed and basked on the hot beach, walked along for half a mile, and then struck back across the shingle into the marsh. And then with a pang of disappointment I saw the first evidence of the intrusion of man into this paradise of solitude, for on a stony spit of ground that ran like some great rib into the amphibious meadows, there stood a small square house built of brick, with a tall flagstaff set up in front of it. It had not caught my eye before, and it seemed an unwarrantable invasion of the emptiness. But perhaps it was not so gross an infringement of it as it appeared, for it wore an indefinable look of desertion, as if man had attempted to domesticate himself here and had failed. As I approached it this impression increased, for the chimney was smokeless, and the closed windows were dim with the film of salt air and the threshold of the closed door was patched with lichen and strewn with débris of withered grasses. I walked twice round it, decided that it was certainly uninhabited, and finally, leaning against the sun-baked wall, ate my lunch.

The glitter and heat of the day were at their height. Warmed and exercised, and invigorated by my bathe, I felt strung to the supreme pitch of physical well-being, and my mind, quite vacant except for these felicitous impressions, followed the example of my body, and basked in an unclouded content. And, I suppose by a sense of the Lucretian luxury of contrast, it began to picture to itself, in order to accentuate these blissful conditions, what this sunlit solitude would be like when some November night began to close in underneath a low, grey sky and a driving storm of sleet. Its solitariness would be turned into an abominable desolation: if from some unconjecturable cause one was forced to spend the night here, how the mind would long for any companionship, how sinister would become the calling of the birds, how weird the whistle of the wind round the cavern of this abandoned habitation. Or would it be just the other way about, and would one only be longing to be assured that the seeming solitude was real, and that no invisible but encroaching presence, soon to be made manifest, was creeping nearer under cover of the dusk, and be shuddering to think that the wail of the wind was not only the wind, but the cry of some discarnate being, and that it was not the curlews who made that melancholy piping? By degrees the edge of thought grew blunt, and melted into inconsequent imaginings, and I fell asleep.

I woke with a start from the trouble of a dream that faded with waking, but felt sure that some noise close at hand had aroused me. And then it came again: it was the footfall of someone moving about inside the deserted house, against the wall of which my back was propped. Up and down it went, then paused and began again; it was like that of a man who waited with impatience for some expected arrival. I noticed also that the footfall had an irregular beat, as if the walker went with a limp. Then in a minute or two the sound ceased altogether.

An odd uneasiness came over me, for I had been so certain that the house was uninhabited. Then turning my head I noticed that in the wall just above me was a window, and the notion, wholly irrational and unfounded, entered my mind that the man inside who tramped was watching me from it. When once that idea got hold of me, it became impossible to sit there in peace any more, and I got up and shovelled into my knapsack my towel and the remains of my meal. I walked a little further down the spit of land which ran out into the marsh, and turning looked at the house again, and again to my eyes it seemed absolutely deserted. But after all, it was no concern of mine and I proceeded on my walk, determining to inquire casually on my return to the hotel who it was that lived in so hermetical a place, and for the present dismissed the matter from my mind.

It was some three hours later that I found myself opposite the house again, after a long wandering walk. I saw that, by making an only slightly longer detour, I could pass close to the house again, and I knew that the sound of those footsteps within it had raised in me a curiosity that I wanted to satisfy. And then, even as I paused, I saw that a man was standing by the door: how he came there I had no idea, for the moment before he had not been there, and he must have come out of the house. He was looking down the path that led through the marsh, shielding his eyes against the sun, and presently he took a step or two forward and he dragged his left leg as he walked, limping heavily. It was his step then which I had heard within, and any mystery about the matter was of my own making. I therefore took the shorter path, and got back to the hotel to find that Jack Granger had just arrived.

We went out again in the gleam of the sunset, and watched the tide sweeping in and pouring up the dykes, until again the great conjuring trick was accomplished, and the stretch of marsh with its fields of sea-lavender was a sheet of shining water. Far away across it stood the house by which I had lunched, and just as we turned Jack pointed to it.

"That's a queer place for a house," he said. "I suppose no one lives there."

"Yes, a lame man," said I, "I saw him to-day. I'm going to ask the hotel porter who he is."

The result of this inquiry was unexpected.

"No; the house has been uninhabited several years," he said. "It used to be a watch-house from which the coastguards signalled if there was a ship in distress, and the lifeboat went out from here. But now the lifeboat and the coastguards are at the end of the Point."

"Then who is the lame man I saw walking about there, and heard inside the house?" I asked.

He looked at me, I thought, queerly.

"I don't know who that could be," he said. "There's no lame man about here to my knowledge."

The effect on Jack of the marshes and their gorgeous emptiness, of the sun and the sea, was precisely what I had anticipated. He vowed that any day spent anywhere than on these beaches and fields of sea-lavender was a day wasted, and proposed that the tour, of which the main object had originally been the golf links of Norfolk, should for the present be cancelled. In particular, it was the birds of this long solitary headland that enchanted him.

"After all, we can play golf anywhere," he said. "There's an oyster-catcher scolding, do you hear?—and how silly to whack a little white ball—ringed plover, but what's that calling as well?—when you can spend the day like this! Oh! don't let us go and bathe yet: I want to wander along that edge of the marsh—ha! there's a company of turnstones, they make a noise like the drawing of a cork—there they are, those little chaps with chestnut-coloured patches! Let's go along the near edge of the marsh, and come out by the house where your lame man lives."

We took, therefore, the path with the longer detour, which I had abandoned last night. I had said nothing to him of what the hotel porter had told me that the house was unlived in, and all he knew was that I had seen a lame man, apparently in occupation there. My reason for not doing so (to make the confession at once) was that I already half believed that the steps I had heard inside, and the lame man I had seen watching outside, did not imply in the porter's sense of the word that the house was occupied, and I wanted to see whether Jack as well as myself would be conscious of any such tokens of a presence there. And then the oddest thing happened.

All the way up to the house his attention was alert on the birds, and in especial on a piping note which was unfamiliar to him. In vain he tried to catch sight of the bird that uttered it, and in vain I tried to hear it. "It doesn't sound like any bird I know," he said, "in fact it doesn't sound like a bird at all, but like some human being whistling. There it is again! Is it possible you don't hear it?"

We were now quite close to the house.

"There must be someone there who is whistling," he said, "it must be your lame man.... Lord! yes, it comes from inside the house. So that's explained, and I hoped it was some new bird. But why can't you hear it?"

"Some people can't hear a bat's squeak," said I.

Jack, satisfied with the explanation, took no more interest in the matter, and we struck across the shingle, bathed and lunched, and tramped on to the tumble of sand dunes in which the Point ended. For a couple of hours we strolled and lazed there in the liquid and sunny air, and reluctantly returned in order to cross the ford before the tide came in. As we retraced our way, I saw coming up from the west a huge continent of cloud: and just as we reached the spit of land on which the house stood, a jagged sword of lightning flickered down to the low-lying hills across the estuary, and a few big raindrops plopped on the shingle.

"We're in for a drenching," he said. "Ha! Let's ask for shelter at your lame man's house. Better run for it!" Already the big drops were falling thickly, and we scuttled across the hundred yards that lay between us and the house, and came to the door just as the sluices of heaven were pulled wide. He rapped on it, but there came no answer; he tried the handle of it, but the door did not yield, and then, by a sudden inspiration, he felt along the top of the lintel and found a key. It fitted into the wards and next moment we stood within.

We found ourselves in a slip of a passage, at the end of which went up the staircase to the floor above. On each side of it was a room, one a kitchen, the other a living-room, but in neither was there any stick of furniture. Discoloured paper was peeling off the walls, the windows were thick with spidery weavings, the air heavy with unventilated damp.

"Your lame man dispenses with the necessities as well as the luxuries of life," said Jack. "A Spartan fellow."

We were standing in the kitchen: outside the hiss of the rain had grown to a roar, and the bleared window was suddenly lit up with a flare of lightning. A crack of thunder answered it, and in the silence that followed there came from just outside, audible now to me, the sound of a piping whistle. Immediately afterwards I heard the door by which we had just entered violently banged, and I remembered that I had left it open.

His eyes met mine.

"But there's no breath of wind," I said. "What made it bang like that?"

"And that was no bird that whistled," said he.

There was the shuffle in the passage outside of a limping step: I could hear the drag of a man's lame foot along the boards.

"He has come in," said Jack.

Yes, he had come in, and who had come in? At that moment not fright, but fear, which is a very different matter, closed in on me. Fright, as I understand it, is an emotion, startling, but not unnerving; you may under the finger of fright spring aside, you may scream, you may shout, you have the command of your muscles. But as that limping step moved down the passage I felt fear, the hand of the nightmare that, as it clutches, paralyses and inhibits not action only, but thought. I waited frozen and speechless for what should happen next.

Exactly opposite the open door of the kitchen in which we stood the step stopped. And then, soundlessly and invisibly, the presence that had made itself manifest to the outward ear, entered. Suddenly I heard Jack's breath rattle in his throat.

"O my God!" he cried in a voice hoarse and strangled, and he threw his left arm across his face as if defending himself, and his right arm shooting out, seemed to hit at something which I could not see, and his fingers crooked themselves as if clutching at that which had evaded his blow. His body was bent back as if resisting some invisible pressure, then lunged forward again, and I heard the noise of a resisting joint, and saw on his throat the shadow (or so it seemed) of a clutching hand. At that some power of movement came back to me, and I remember hurling myself at the empty space between him and me, and felt under my grip the shape of a shoulder and heard on the boards of the floor the slip and scoop of a foot. Something invisible, now a shoulder, now an arm, struggled in my grasp, and I heard a panting respiration that was not Jack's, nor mine, and now and then in my face I felt a hot breath that stank of corruption and decay. And all the time this physical contention was symbolical only: what he and I wrestled with was not a thing of flesh and blood, but some awful spiritual presence. And then….

There was nothing. The ghostly invasion ceased as suddenly as it had begun, and there was Jack's face gleaming with sweat close to mine, as we stood with dropped arms opposite each other in an empty room, with the rain beating on the roof and the gutters chuckling. No word passed between us, but next moment we were out in the pelting rain, running for the ford. The deluge was sweet to my soul, it seemed to wash away that horror of great darkness and that odour of corruption in which we had been plunged.

Now I have no certain explanation to give of the experience which has here been shortly recounted, and the reader may or may not connect with it a story that I heard a week or two later on my return to London.

A friend of mine and I had been dining at my house one evening, and we had discussed a murder trial then going on of which the papers were full.

"It isn't only the atrocity that attracts," he said, "I think it is the place where the murder occurs that is the cause of the interest in it. A murder at Brighton or Margate or Ramsgate, any place which the public associates with pleasure trips, attracts them because they know the place and can visualise the scene. But when there is a murder at some small unknown spot, which they have never heard of, there is no appeal to their imagination. Last spring, for instance, there was the murder at that small village on the coast of Norfolk. I've forgotten the name of the place, though I was in Norwich at the time of the trial and was present in court. It was one of the most awful stories I ever heard, as ghastly and sensational as this last affair, but it didn't attract the smallest attention. Odd that I can't remember the name of the place when all the rest is so vivid to me!"

"Tell me about it," I said; "I never heard of it."

"Well, there was this little village, and just outside it was a farm, owned by a man called John Beardsley. He lived there with his only daughter, an unmarried woman of about thirty, a good-looking, sensible creature apparently, the last in the world you would have thought to do anything unexpected. There worked at the farm as a day labourer a young fellow called Alfred Maldon, who, in the trial of which I am speaking, was the prisoner. He had one of the most dreadful faces I ever saw, a cat-like receding forehead, a broad, short nose, and a great red sensual mouth, always on the grin. He seemed positively to enjoy being the central figure round whom all the interest of those ghoulish women who thronged the court was concentrated, and when he shambled into the witness-box——"

"Shambled?" I asked.

"Yes, he was lame, his left foot dragged along the floor as he walked. As he shambled into the witness-box he nodded and smiled to the judge, and clapped his counsel on the shoulder, and leered at the gallery…. He worked on the farm, as I was saying, doing jobs that were within his capacity, among which was certain housework, carrying coals and what-not, for John Beardsley, though very well-off, kept no servant, and this daughter Alice— that was her name—ran the house. And what must she do but fall in love, it was no less than that, with this monstrous and misshapen fellow. One afternoon her father came home unexpectedly and caught them together in the parlour, kissing and cuddling. He turned the man out of the house, neck and crop, gave him his week's wages, and dismissed him, threatening him with a fine thrashing if he ever caught him hanging about the place. He forbade his daughter ever to speak to him again, and in order to keep watch over her, got in a woman from the village who would be there all day while he was out on the farm.

"Young Maldon, deprived of his job, tried to get work in the village, but none would employ him, for he was a black-tempered fellow ready to pick a quarrel with anyone, and an unpleasant opponent, for, with all his lameness, he was of immense muscular strength. For some weeks he idled about in the village getting a chance job occasionally and no doubt, as you will see, Alice Beardsley managed to meet him. The village—its name still escapes me—

lay on the edge of a big tidal estuary, full at high water, but on the ebb of a broad stretch of marsh and sand and mud-banks, beyond which ran a long belt of shingle that formed the seaward side of the estuary. On it stood a disused coastguard house, a couple of miles away from the village, and in as lonely a place as you would find anywhere in England. At low tide there was a shallow ford across to it, and in the sand-banks round about it some beds of cockle. Maldon, unable to get regular work, took to cockle-digging, and during the summer when the tide was low, Alice (it was no new thing with her) used to go over the ford to the beach beyond and bathe. She would go across the sand-banks where the cockle-diggers, Maldon among them, were at work, and if he whistled as she passed that was the signal between them that he would slip away presently and join her at the disused coastguard house, and there throughout the summer they used to meet.

"As the weeks went on her father saw the change that was coming in her, and suspecting the cause, often left his work and, hidden behind some sea-bank, used to watch her. One day he saw her cross the ford, and soon after she had passed he saw Maldon, recognisable from a long way off by his dragging leg, follow her. He went up the path to the coastguard house, and entered. At that John Beardsley crossed the ford, and hiding in the bushes near the house, saw Alice coming back from her bathe. The house was off the direct path to the ford, but she went round that way, and the door was opened to her, and closed behind her. He found them together, and mad with rage attacked the man. They fought and Maldon got him down and then and there in front of his daughter strangled him.

"The girl went off her head, and is in the asylum at Norwich now. She sits all day by the window whistling. The man was hanged."

"Was Riddington the name of the village?" I asked.

"Yes. Riddington, of course," he said. "I can't think how I forgot it."

VI

NABOTH'S VINEYARD

Ralph Hatchard had for the last twenty years been making a very good income at the Bar; no one could marshal facts so tellingly as he, no one could present a case to a jury in so persuasive and convincing a way, nor make them see the situation he pictured to them with so sympathetic an eye. He disdained to awaken sentiment by moving appeals to humanity, for he had not, either in his private or his public life, any use for mercy, but demanded mere justice for his client. Many were the cases in which, not by distorting facts, but merely by focusing them for the twelve intelligent men whom he addressed, he had succeeded in making them look through the telescope of his mind, and see at the end of it precisely what he wished them to see. But if he had been asked of which out of all his advocacies he was most intellectually proud, he would probably have mentioned one in which that advocacy had not been successful. This was in the famous Wraxton case of seven years ago, in which he had defended a certain solicitor, Thomas Wraxton, on a charge of embezzlement and conversion to his own use of the money of a client.

As the case was presented by the prosecution, it seemed as if any defence would merely waste the time of the court, but when the speech for the defence was concluded, most of them who heard it, not the public alone, but the audience of trained legal minds, would probably have betted (had betting been permitted in a court of justice) that Thomas Wraxton would be acquitted. But the twelve intelligent men were among the minority, and after being absent from court for three hours had brought in a verdict of guilty. A sentence of seven years was passed on Thomas Wraxton, and his counsel, thoroughly disgusted that so much ingenuity should have been thrown away, felt, ever afterward, a sort of contemptuous irritation with him. The irritation was rendered more acute by an interview he had with Wraxton after sentence had been passed. His client raged and stormed at him for the stupidity and lack of skill he had shown in his defence.

Hatchard was a bachelor; he had little opinion of women as companions, and it was enough for him in town when his day's work was over to take his dinner at the club, and after a stern rubber or two at bridge, to retire to his flat, and more often than not work at some case in which he was engaged till the small hours. Apart from the dinner-table and the card-table, the only companion he wanted was an opponent at golf for Saturday and Sunday, when he went down for his week-end to the seaside links at Scarling. There was a pleasant dormy-house in the town, at which he put up, and in the summer he was accustomed to spend the greater part of the long vacation here, renting a house in the neighbourhood. His only near relation was a brother who had a Civil Service appointment at Bareilly, in the North-West province of India, whom he had not seen for some years, for he spent the hot season in the hills and but seldom came to England.

Hatchard got from acquaintances all the friendship that he needed, and though he was a solitary man, he was by no means to be described as a lonely one. For loneliness implies the knowledge that a man is alone, and his wish that it were otherwise. Hatchard knew he was alone, but preferred it. His golf and his bridge of an evening gave him all the companionship he needed; a further recreation of his was botany. "Plants are good to look at, they're interesting to study, and they don't bore you by unwished-for conversation" would have been his manner of accounting for so unexpected a hobby. He intended, when he retired from practice, to buy a house with a good garden in some country town, where he could enjoy at leisure this trinity of innocuous amusements. Till then, there was no use in having a garden from which his work would sever him for the greater part of the year.

He always took the same house at Scarling when he came to spend his long vacation there. It suited him admirably, for it was within a few doors of the local club, where he could get a rubber in the evening, and find a match at golf for next day, and the motor omnibuses that plied along the seaside road to the links passed his door. He had long ago settled in his mind that Scarling was to be the home of his late and leisured years, and of all the houses in that compact mediæval little town the one which he most coveted lay close to that which he was now accustomed to take for the summer months. Opposite his windows ran the long red-brick wall of its garden, and from his bedroom above he could look over this and see the amenities which in its present proprietorship seemed so sadly undervalued.

An acre of lawn with a gnarled and sprawling mulberry tree lay there, a pergola of rambler-roses separated this from the kitchen garden, and all round in the shelter of the walls which defended them from the chill northerly and easterly blasts lay deep flower beds. A paved terrace faced the garden side of Telford House, but weeds were sprouting there, the grass of the lawn had been suffered to grow long and rank, and the flower beds were an untended jungle. The house, too, seemed exactly what would suit him, it was of Queen Anne date, and he could conjecture the square panelled rooms within. He had been to the house-agent's in Scarling to ask if there was any chance of obtaining it, and had directed him to make inquiries of the occupying tenant or proprietor as to whether he had any thoughts of getting rid of it to a purchaser who was prepared to negotiate at once for it. But it appeared that it had only been bought some six years ago by the present owner, Mrs. Pringle, when she came to live at Scarling, and she had no idea of parting with it.

Ralph Hatchard, when he was at Scarling, took no part whatever in the local life and society of the place except in so far as he encountered it among the men whom he met in the card-room of the club and out at the links, and it appeared that Mrs. Pringle was as recluse as he. Once or twice in casual conversation mention had been made by one or another of her house or its owner, but nothing was forthcoming about her. He learned that when she had come there first, the usual country-town civilities had been paid her, but she either did not return the call or soon suffered the acquaintanceship to drop, and at the present time she appeared to see nobody except occasionally the vicar of the church or his wife. Hatchard made no particular note of all this, and did not construct any such hypothesis as might be supposed to divert the vagrant thoughts of a legal mind by picturing her as a woman hiding from justice or from the exposure that justice had already subjected her to. As far as he was aware he had never set eyes on her, nor had he any object in wishing to do so, as long as she was not willing to part with her house; it was sufficient for a man who was not in the least inquisitive (except when conducting a cross-examination) to suppose that she liked her own company well enough to dispense with that of others. Plenty of sensible folk did that, and he thought no worse of them for it.

More than six years had now elapsed since the Wraxton trial, and Hatchard was spending the last days of the long vacation at the house that overlooked that Naboth's vineyard of a garden. The day was one of squealing wind and driving rain, and even he, who usually defied the elements to stop his couple of rounds of golf, had not gone out to the links to-day. Towards evening, however, it cleared, and he set out to get a mouthful of fresh air and a little exercise, and returned just about sunset past the house he coveted. There were two women standing on the threshold as he approached, one of them hatless, and it came into his mind that here, no doubt, was the retiring Mrs. Pringle. She stood side-face to him for that moment, and at once he knew that he had seen her before; her face and her carriage were perfectly but remotely familiar to him. Then she turned and saw him; she gave him but one glance, and without pause went back into the house and shut the door. The sight he had of her was but instantaneous, but sufficient to convince him not only that he had seen her before, but that she was in no way desirous of seeing him again.

Mrs. Grampound, the vicar's wife, had been talking to her, and Hatchard raised his hat, for he had been introduced to her one day when he had been playing golf with her husband. He alluded to the malignity of the weather, which, after being wet all day, was clearly going to be uselessly fine all night.

"And that lady, I suppose," he said, "with whom you were speaking, was Mrs. Pringle? A widow, perhaps? One does not meet her husband at the club."

"No; she is not a widow," said Mrs. Grampound. "Indeed, she told me just now that she expected her husband home before long. He has been out in India for some years."

"Indeed! I heard only to-day from my brother, who is also in India. I expect him home in the spring for six months' leave. Perhaps I shall find that he knows Mr. Pringle."

They had come to his house, and he turned in. Somehow, Mrs. Pringle had ceased to be merely the owner of the house he so much desired. She was somebody else, and good though his memory was, he could not recall where he had met her before. He could not in the least remember the sound of her voice, perhaps he had never heard it. But he knew her face.

During the winter he was often down at Scarling again for his week-ends, and now he was definitely intending to retire from practice before the summer. He had made sufficient money to live with all possible comfort, and he was certainly beginning to feel the strain of his work. His memory was not quite what it had been, and he who had been robust as a piece of ironwork all his life, had several times been in the doctor's hands. It was clearly time, if he was going to enjoy the long evening of life, to begin doing so while the capacity for enjoyment was still unimpaired, and not linger on at work till his health suffered. He could not concentrate as he had been used; even when he was most occupied in his own argument the train of his thought would grow dim, and through it, as if through a mist, vague images of thought would fleetingly appear, images not fully tangible to his mind, and evade him before he could grasp them.

That logical constructive brain of his was certainly getting tired with its years of incessant work, and knowing that, he longed more than ever to have done with business, and more vividly than ever he saw himself established in that particular house and garden at Scarling. The thought of it bid fair to become an obsession with him; he began to look upon Mrs. Pringle as an enemy standing in the way of the fulfilment of his dream, and still he cudgelled his brain to think when and where and how he had seen her before. Sometimes he seemed close to the solution of that conundrum, but just as he pounced on it, it slipped away again, like some object in the dusk.

He was down there one week-end in March and instead of playing golf, spent his Saturday morning in looking over a couple of houses which were for sale. His brother, whom he now expected back in a week or two, and who, like himself, was a bachelor, would be living with him all the summer, and now at last despairing of getting the house he wanted, he must resign himself to the inevitable, and get some other permanent home. One of these two houses, he thought, would do for him fairly well, and after viewing it he went to the house agent's and secured the first refusal of it, with a week in which to make up his mind.

"I shall almost certainly purchase it," he said, "for I suppose there is still no chance of my getting Telford House."

The agent shook his head.

"I'm afraid not, sir," he said. "Mr. Pringle, you may have heard, has come home, and lives there now."

As he left the office an idea occurred to him. Though Mrs. Pringle might not, when living there alone, have felt disposed to face the inconvenience of moving, it was possible that a firm and adequate offer made to her husband might effect something. He had only just come there, it was not to be supposed that he had any very strong attachment to the house, and a definite offer of so many thousand pounds down might perhaps induce him to give it up. Hatchard determined, before definitely purchasing another house, to make a final effort to get that on which his heart was set.

He went straight to Telford House and rang. He gave the maid his card, asking if he could see Mr. Pringle, and at that moment a man came into the little hall from the door into the garden, and seeing someone there paused as he entered. He was a tall fellow, but bent; and walked limpingly with the aid of a stick. He wore a short grey beard and moustache, his eyes were sunk deep below the overhanging brows.

Hatchard gave one glance at him, and a curious thing happened. Instantly there sprang into his mind not, first of all, the knowledge of who this man was, but the knowledge which had so long evaded him. He remembered everything: Mrs. Pringle's white, drawn face as she looked at the jury filing into the box again at the end of their consultation, in which they had decided the guilt or the innocence of Thomas Wraxton. No wonder she was all suspense and anxiety, for it was her husband's fate that was being decided. And then, a moment afterwards, he could trace in the face of the man who stood at the garden door the shattered identity of him who had stood in the dock. But had it not been for his wife, he thought he would not have recognised him, so terribly had suffering changed him. He looked very ill, and the high colour in his face clearly pointed to a weakness of the heart rather than a vigorous circulation.

Hatchard turned to him. He did not intend to use his deadliest weapon unless it was necessary. But at that moment he told himself that Telford House would be his.

"You will excuse me, Mr. Pringle," he said, "for calling on you so unceremoniously. My name is Hatchard, Ralph Hatchard, and I should be most grateful if you would let me have a few minutes' conversation with you."

Pringle took a step forward. He told himself that he had not been recognised; that was no wonder. But the shock of the encounter had left him trembling.

"Certainly," he said; "shall we go into my room here?"

The two went into a little sitting-room close by the front door.

"My business is quite short," said Hatchard. "I am on the look-out for a house here, and of all the houses in Scarling yours is the one which I have long wanted. I am willing to pay you £6,000 pounds for it. I may add that there is an extremely pleasant house, which I have the option to purchase, which you can obtain for half that sum."

Pringle shook his head.

"I am not thinking of parting with my house," he said.

"If it is a matter of price," said Hatchard, "I am willing to make it £6,500."

"It is not a matter of price," said Pringle. "The house suits my wife and me, and it is not for sale."

Hatchard paused a moment. The man had been his client, but a guilty and a very ungrateful one.

"I am quite determined to get this house, Mr. Pringle," he said. "You will make, I feel sure, a very handsome profit by accepting the price I offer, and if you are attached to Scarling you will be able to purchase a very convenient residence!"

"The house is not for sale," said Pringle.

Hatchard looked at him closely.

"You will be more comfortable in the other house," he said. "You will live there, I assure you, in peace and security, and I hope you will spend many pleasant years there as Mr. Pringle from India. That will be better than being known as Mr. Thomas Wraxton, of His Majesty's prison."

The wretched man shrunk into a mere nerveless heap in his chair, and wiped his forehead.

"You know me, then?" he said.

"Intimately, I may say," retorted Hatchard.

Five minutes later, Hatchard left the house. He had in his pocket Mr. Pringle's acceptance of his offer of £6,500 for Telford House with possession in a month's time. That night the doctor was hurriedly sent for to Telford House, but his skill was of no avail against the heart attack which proved fatal to his patient.

Ralph Hatchard was sitting on the flagged terrace on the garden side of his newly-acquired house one warm evening in May. He had spent his morning on the links with his brother Francis, his afternoon in the garden, weeding and planting, and now he was glad enough to sprawl in his low easy basket-chair and glance at the paper which he had not yet read. He had been a month here, and looking back through his happy and busy life, he could not recollect having ever been busier and happier. It was said, how falsely he now knew, that if a man gave up his work, he often went downhill both in mind and body, growing stout and lazy and losing that interest in life which keeps old-age in the background, but the very opposite had been his own experience. He played his golf and his bridge with just as much zest as when they had been the recreation from his work, and he found time now for serious reading. He gardened, too, you might say with gluttony; awaking in the morning found him refreshed and eager for the pleasurable toil and exercise of the day, and every evening found him ready for bed and long dreamless sleep.

He sat, alone for the time being, content to take his ease and glance at the news. Even now he gave but a cursory attention to it and his eye wandered over the lawn, and the long-neglected flower-beds, which the joint labours of the gardener and himself were quickly bringing back into orderly cultivation. The lawn must be cut to-morrow, and there were some late-flowering roses to be planted.... Then perhaps he dozed a little, for though he had heard no one approach, there was the sound of steps somewhere at his back quite close to him, and the tapping of a stick on the paving-stones of the terrace. He did not look round, for of course it must be Francis returned from his shopping; he had occasional twinges of rheumatism which made him a little lame, but Ralph had not noticed till to-day that he limped like that.

61

"Is your rheumatism bothering you, Francis?" he said, still not looking round. There was no answer and he turned his head. The terrace was quite empty: neither his brother nor anyone else was there.

For the moment he was startled: then he was aware that he certainly had been dozing, for his paper had slipped off his knee without his noticing it. No doubt this impression was the fag-end of some dream. Confirmation of that immediately came, for there in the street outside was the noise of a tapping footfall; it was that no doubt that had mingled itself with some only half-waking impression. He had dreamed, too, now that he came to think about it; he had dreamed something about poor Wraxton. What it was he could not recollect, beyond that Wraxton was angry with him and railed at him just as he had done after that long sentence had been passed on him.

The sun had set, and there was a slight chill in the air which caused him a moment's goose-flesh. So getting out of his basket-chair he took a turn along the gravel path which bordered the lawn, his eye dwelling with satisfaction on the labours of the day. The bed had been smothered in weeds a week ago; now there was not a weed to be seen on it.... Ah! just one; that small piece of chickweed had evaded notice, and he bent down to root it up. At that moment he heard the limping step again, not in the street at all, but close to him on the terrace, and the basket-chair creaked, as if someone had sat down in it. But again the terrace was void of occupants, and his chair empty.

It would have been strange indeed if a man so hard-headed and practical as Hatchard had allowed himself to be disturbed by an echoing stone and a creaking chair, and it was with no effort that he dismissed them. He had plenty to occupy him without that, but once or twice in the next week he received impressions which he definitely chucked into the lumber-room of his mind as among the things for which he had no use. One morning, for instance, after the gardener had gone to his dinner, he thought he saw him standing on the far side of the mulberry tree, half screened by the foliage. He took the trouble to walk round the tree on this occasion, but found no one there, neither his gardener nor any other, and coming back to the place where he had received this impression, he saw (and was secretly relieved to see) that a splash of light on the wall beyond might have tricked him into constructing a human figure there. But though his waking moments were still untroubled he began to sleep badly, and when he slept to be the prey of vivid and terrible dreams, from which he would awake in disordered panic.

The recollection of these was vague, but always he had been pursued by something invisible and angry that had come in from the garden, and was limping swiftly after him upstairs and along the passage at the end of which his room lay. Invariably, too, he just escaped into his room before the pursuer clutched him, and banged his door, the crash of which (in his dream) awoke him. Then he would turn on the light, and, despite himself, cast a glance at the door, and the oblong of glass above it which gave light to this dark end of the passage, as if to be sure that nothing was looking through it;

and once, upbraiding himself for his cowardice, he had gone to the door and opened it, and turned on the light in the passage outside. But it was empty.

By day he was master of himself, though he knew that his self-control was becoming a matter that demanded effort. Often and often, though still nothing was visible, he heard the limping steps on the terrace and along the weeded gravel-path; but instead of becoming used to so harmless an hallucination, which seemed to usher in nothing further, he grew to fear it. But until a certain day, it was only in the garden that he heard that step....

July was now half way through, when a broiling morning was succeeded by a storm that raced up from the south. Thunder had been remotely muttering for an hour or two, and now as he worked on the garden beds, the first large tepid drops of rain warned him that the downpour was imminent, and he had scarcely reached the door into the hall when it descended. The sluices of heaven were opened, and thick as a tropical tempest the rain splashed and steamed on the terrace. As he stood in the doorway, he heard the limping step come slowly and unhurried through the deluge, and up to the door where he stood. But it did not pause there; he felt something invisible push by him, he heard the steps limp across the hall within, and the door of the sitting-room, where he had sat one morning in March and watched Wraxton's tremulous signature traced on the paper, swing open and close again.

Ralph Hatchard stood steady as a rock, holding himself firmly in hand. "So it's come into the house," he said to himself. "So it's come in—ha!—out of the rain," he added. But he knew, when that unseen presence had pushed by him to the door, that at that moment terror real and authentic had touched some inmost fibre of him. That touch had quitted him now; he could reassert his dominion over himself, and be steady, but as surely as that unseen presence had entered the house, so surely had fear found entry into his soul.

All the afternoon the rain continued; golf and gardening were alike out of the question, and presently he went round to the club to find a rubber of bridge. He was wise to be occupied, occupation was always good, especially for one who now had in his mind a prohibited area where it was better not to graze. For something invisible and angry had come into the house, and he must starve it into quitting it again, not by facing it and defying it, but by the subtler and the safe process of denying and disregarding it. A man's soul was his own enclosed garden, nothing could obtain admittance there without his invitation and permission. He must forget it till he could afford to laugh at the fantastic motive of its existence.... Besides, the perception of it was purely subjective, so he argued to himself: it had no real existence outside himself; his brother, for instance, and the servants were quite unaware of the limping steps that so constantly were heard by him. The invisible phantom was the product of some derangement of his own senses, some misfunction of the nerves. To convince himself of that, as he passed through the hall on his way to the club, he went into the room into which the limping steps had passed. Of course there was nothing there, it was just the small quiet, unoccupied sitting-room that he knew.

There was some brisk bridge, which he enjoyed in his usual grim and magisterial manner, and dusk, hastened on by the thick pall of cloud which still overset the sky, was falling when he got back home again. He went into the panelled sitting-room looking out on the garden, and found Francis there, cheery and robust. The lamps were lit, but the blinds and curtains not yet drawn, and outside an illuminated oblong of light lay across the terrace.

"Well, pleasant rubbers?" asked Francis.

"Very decent," said Ralph. "You've not been out?"

"No, why go out in the rain, when there's a house to keep you dry? By the way, have you seen your visitor?"

Ralph knew that his heart checked and missed a beat. Had that which was invisible to him become visible to another?... Then he pulled himself together; why shouldn't there have been a visitor to see him?

"No," he said, "who was it?"

Francis beat out his pipe against the bars of the grate.

"I'm sure I don't know," he said. "But ten minutes ago, I passed through the hall, and there was a man sitting on a chair there. I asked him what he wanted, and he said he was waiting to see you. I supposed it was somebody who had called by appointment, and I said you would no doubt be in presently, and suggested that he would be more comfortable in that little sitting-room than waiting in the hall. So I showed him in there, and shut the door on him."

Ralph rang the bell.

"Who is it who has called to see me?" he asked the parlourmaid.

"Nobody, sir, that I know of," she said; "I haven't let anyone in!"

"Well, somebody has called," he said, "and he's in the little sitting-room near the front door. Just see who it is; and ask him his name and his business."

He paused a moment, making a call on his courage.

"No; I'll go myself," he said.

He came back in a few seconds.

"Whoever it was, he has gone," he said. "I suppose he got tired of waiting. What was he like, Francis?"

"I couldn't see him very distinctly, for it was pretty dark in the hall. He had a grey beard, I saw that, and he walked with a limp."

Ralph turned to the window to pull down the blind. At that moment he heard a step on the terrace outside, and there stepped into the illuminated oblong the figure of a man. He leaned heavily on a stick as he walked, and came close up to the window, his eyes blazing with some devilish fury, his mouth mumbling and working in his beard.... Then down came the blind, and the rattle of the curtain-rings along the pole followed.

The evening passed quietly enough: the two brothers dined together, and played a few hands at piquet afterwards, and before going up to bed looked out into the garden to see what promise the weather gave. But the rain still dripped, and the air was sultry with storm. Lightning quivered now and again in the west, and in one of these blinks Francis suddenly pointed towards the mulberry-tree.

"Who is that?" he said.

"I saw no one," said Ralph.

Once more the lightning made things visible, and Francis laughed.

"Ah! I see," he said. "It's only the trunk of the tree and that grey patch of sky through the leaves. I could have sworn there was somebody there. That's a good example of how ghost stories arise. If it had not been for that second flash, we should have searched the garden, and, finding nobody, I should have been convinced I had seen a ghost!"

"Very sound," said Ralph.

He lay long awake that night, listening to the hiss of the rain on the shrubs outside his window, and to a footfall that moved about the house....

The next few days passed without the renewal of any direct manifestations of the presence that had entered the house. But the cessation of it brought no relief to the pressure of some force that seemed combing in over Ralph Hatchard's mind. When he was out on the links or at the club it relaxed its hold on him, but the moment he entered his door it gripped him again. It mattered not that he neither saw nor heard anything for which there was no normal and material explanation; the power, whatever it was, was about his path and about his bed, driving terror into him. He confessed to strange lassitude and depression, and eventually yielded to his brother's advice, and made an appointment with his doctor in town for next day.

"Much the wisest course," said Francis. "Doctors are a splendid institution. Whenever I feel down I go and see one, and he always tells me there's nothing the matter. In consequence I feel better at once. Going up to bed? I shall follow in half an hour. There's an amusing tale I'm in the middle of."

"Put out the light then," said Ralph, "and I'll tell the servants they can go to bed."

The half-hour lengthened into an hour, and it was not much before midnight that Francis finished his tale. There was a switch in the hall to be turned off, and another half-way up the stairs. As his finger was on this, he looked up to see that the passage above was still lit, and saw, leaning on the banister at the top of the stairs the figure of a man. He had already put out the light on the stairs, and this figure was silhouetted in black against the bright background of the lit passage. For a moment he supposed that it must be his brother, and then the man turned, and he saw that he was grey-bearded, and limped as he walked.

"Who the devil are you?" cried Francis.

He got no reply, but the figure moved away up the passage, at the end of which was Ralph's room. He was now in full pursuit after it, but before he had traversed one half of the passage it was already at the end of it, and had gone into his brother's room. Strangely bewildered and alarmed, he followed, knocked on Ralph's door, calling him loudly by name, and turned the handle to enter. But the door did not yield for all his pushing, and again "Ralph! Ralph!" he called aloud, but there was no answer.

Above the door was a glass pane that gave light to the passage, and looking up he saw that this was black, showing that the room was in darkness within. But even as he looked, it started into light, and simultaneously from inside there rose a cry of mortal agony.

"Oh, my God, my God!" rang out his brother's voice, and again that cry of agony resounded.

Then there was another voice, speaking low and angry....

"No, no!" yelled Ralph again, and again in a panic of fear Francis put his shoulder to the door and strove quite in vain to open it, for it seemed as if the door had become a part of the solid wall.

Once more that cry of terror burst out, and then, whatever was taking place within, was all over, for there was dead silence. The door which had resisted his most frenzied efforts now yielded to him, and he entered.

His brother was in bed, his legs drawn up close under him, and his hands, resting on his knees, seemed to be attempting to beat off some terrible intruder. His body was pressed against the wall at the head of the bed, and the face was a mask of agonised horror and fruitless entreaty. But the eyes were already glazed in death, and before Francis could reach the bed the body had toppled over and lay inert and lifeless. Even as he looked, he heard a limping step go down the passage outside.

VII

EXPIATION

Philip Stuart and I, unattached and middle-aged persons, had for the last four or five years been accustomed to spend a month or six weeks together in the summer, taking a furnished house in some part of the country, which, by an absence of attractive pursuits, was not likely to be over-run by gregarious holiday-makers. When, as the season for getting out of London draws near, and we scan the advertisement columns which set forth the charms and the cheapness of residences to be let for August, and see the mention of tennis-clubs and esplanades and admirable golf-links within a stone's throw of the proposed front door, our offended and disgusted eyes instantly wander to the next item.

For the point of a holiday, according to our private heresy, is not to be entertained and occupied and jostled by glad crowds, but to have nothing to do, and no temptation which might lead to any unseasonable activity. London has held employments and diversion enough; we want to be without both. But vicinity to the sea is desirable, because it is easier to do nothing by the sea than anywhere else, and because bathing and basking on the shore cannot be considered an employment but only an apotheosis of loafing. A garden also is a requisite, for that tranquillises any fidgety notion of going for a walk.

In pursuance of this sensible policy we had this year taken a house on the south coast of Cornwall, for a relaxing climate conduces to laziness. It was too far off for us to make any personal inspection of it, but a perusal of the modestly-worded advertisement carried conviction. It was close to the sea; the village Polwithy, outside which it was situated, was remote and, as far as we knew, unknown; it had a garden, and there was attached to it a cook-housekeeper who made for simplification. No mention of golf-links or attractive resorts in the neighbourhood defiled the bald and terse specification, and though there was a tennis-court in the garden, there was no clause that bound the tenants to use it. The owner was a Mrs. Hearne, who had been living abroad, and our business was transacted with a house-agent in Falmouth.

To make our household complete, Philip sent down a parlourmaid, and I a housemaid, and after leaving them a day in which to settle in, we followed. There was a six-mile drive from the station across high uplands, and at the end a long steady descent into a narrow valley, cloven between the hills, that grew ever more luxuriant in verdure as we descended. Great trees of fuchsia spread up to the eaves of the thatched cottages which stood by the wayside, and a stream, embowered in green thickets, ran babbling through the centre of it. Presently we came to the village, no more than a dozen houses, built of the grey stone of the district, and on a shelf just above it a tiny church with parsonage adjoining. High above us now flamed the gorse-clad slopes of the hills on each side, and now the valley opened out at its lower end, and the still warm air was spiced and renovated by the breeze that drew up it from the sea. Then round a sharp angle of the road we came alongside a stretch of brick wall, and stopped at an iron gate above which flowed a riot of rambler rose.

It seemed hardly credible that it was this of which that terse and laconic advertisement had spoken. I had pictured something of villa-ish kind, yellow bricked perhaps, with a roof of purplish slate, a sitting-room one side of the entrance, a dining-room the other; with a tiled hall and a pitch-pine staircase, and instead, here was this little gem of an early Georgian manor house, mellow and gracious, with mullioned windows and a roof of stone slabs. In front of it was a paved terrace, below which blossomed a herbaceous border, tangled and tropical, with no inch of earth visible through its luxuriance.

67

Inside, too, was fulfilment of this fair exterior: a broad-balustered staircase led up from the odiously-entitled "lounge hall," which I had pictured as a medley of Benares ware and saddle-bagged sofas, but which proved to be cool, broad and panelled, with a door opposite that through which we entered, leading on to the further area of garden at the back. There was the advertised but innocuous tennis court, bordered on the length of its far side by a steep grass bank, along which was planted a row of limes, once pollarded, but now allowed to develop at will. Thick boughs, some fourteen or fifteen feet from the ground, interlaced with each other, forming an arcaded row; above them, where Nature had been permitted to go her own way, the trees broke into feathered and honey-scented branches. Beyond lay a small orchard climbing upwards, above that the hillside rose more steeply, in broad spaces of short-cropped turf and ablaze with gorse, the Cornish gorse that flowers all the year round, and spreads its sunshine from January to December.

There was time for a stroll through this perfect little domain before dinner, and for a short interview with the housekeeper, a quiet capable-looking woman, slightly aloof, as is the habit of her race, from strangers and foreigners, for so the Cornish account the English, but who proved herself at the repast that followed to be as capable as she appeared. The evening closed in hot and still, and after dinner we took chairs out on to the terrace in front of the house.

"Far the best place we've struck yet," observed Philip. "Why did no one say Polwithy before?"

"Because nobody had ever heard of it, luckily," said I.

"Well, I'm a Polwithian. At least I am in spirit. But how aware Mrs.—Mrs. Criddle made me feel that I wasn't really."

Philip's profession, a doctor of obscure nervous diseases, has made him preternaturally acute in the diagnosis of what other people feel, and for some reason, quite undefined, I wanted to know what exactly he meant by this. I was in sympathy with his feeling, but I could not analyse it.

"Describe your symptoms," I said.

"I have. When she came up and talked to us, and hoped we should be comfortable, and told us that she would do her best, she was just gossiping. Probably it was perfectly true gossip. But it wasn't she. However, as that's all that matters, there's no reason why we should probe further."

"Which means that you have," I said.

"No; it means that I tried to and couldn't. She gave me an extraordinary sense of her being aware of something, which we knew nothing of; of being on a plane which we couldn't imagine. I constantly meet such people; they aren't very rare. I don't mean that there's anything the least uncanny about them, or that they know things that are uncanny. They are simply aloof, as hard to understand as your dog or your cat. She would find us equally aloof if she succeeded in analysing her sensations about us, but like a sensible woman she probably feels not the smallest interest in us. She is there to bake and to boil, and we are there to eat her bakings and appreciate her boilings."

The subject dropped, and we sat on in the dusk that was rapidly deepening into night. The door into the hall was open at our backs, and a panel of light from the lamps within was cast out on to the terrace. Wandering moths, invisible in the darkness, suddenly became manifest as they fluttered into this illumination, and vanished again as they passed out of it. One moment they were there, living things with life and motion of their own, the next they had quite disappeared. How inexplicable that would be, I thought, if one did not know from long familiarity, that light of the appropriate sort and strength is needed to make material objects visible.

Philip must have been following precisely the same train of thought, for his voice broke in, carrying it a little further.

"Look at that moth," he said, "and even while you look it has gone like a ghost, even as like a ghost it appeared. Light made it visible. And there are other sorts of light, interior psychical light which similarly makes visible the beings which people the darkness of our blindness."

Just as he spoke I thought for the moment that I heard the tingle of a telephone bell. It sounded very faintly, and I could not have sworn that I had actually heard it. At the most it gave one staccato little summons and was silent again.

"Is there a telephone in the house?" I asked "I haven't noticed one."

"Yes, by the door into the back garden," said he. "Do you want to telephone?"

"No, but I thought I heard it ring. Didn't you?"

He shook his head; then smiled.

"Ah, that was it," he said.

Certainly now there was the clink of glass, rather bell-like, as the parlourmaid came out of the dining-room with a tray of syphon and decanter, and my reasonable mind was quite content to accept this very probable explanation. But behind that, quite unreasonably, some little obstinate denizen of my consciousness rejected it. It told me that what I had heard was like the moth that came out of darkness and went on into darkness again....

My room was at the back of the house, overlooking the lawn tennis-court, and presently I went up to bed. The moon had risen, and the lawn lay in bright illumination bordered by a strip of dark shadow below the pollarded limes. Somewhere along the hillside an owl was foraging, softly hooting, and presently it swept whitely across the lawn. No sound is so intensely rural, yet none, to my mind, so suggests a signal. But it seemed to signal nothing, and, tired with the long hot journey, and soothed by the deep tranquillity of the place, I was soon asleep. But often during the night I woke, though never to more than a dozing dreamy consciousness of where I was, and each time I had the notion that some slight noise had roused me, and each time I found myself listening to hear whether the tingle of a telephone bell was the cause of my disturbance. There came no repetition of it, and again I slept, and again I woke with drowsy attention for the sound which I felt I expected, but never heard.

Daylight banished these imaginations, but though I must have slept many hours all told, for these wakings had been only brief and partial, I was aware of a certain weariness, as if though my bodily senses had been rested, some part of me had been wakeful and watching all night. This was fanciful enough to disregard, and certainly during the day I forgot it altogether. Soon after breakfast we went down to the sea, and a short ramble along a shingly shore brought us to a sandy cove framed in promontories of rock that went down into deep water. The most fastidious connoisseur in bathing could have pictured no more ideal scene for his operations, for with hot sand to bask on and rocks to plunge from, and a limpid ocean and a cloudless sky, there was indeed no lacuna in perfection. All morning we loafed here, swimming and sunning ourselves, and for the afternoon there was the shade of the garden, and a stroll later on up through the orchard and to the gorse-clad hillside. We came back through the churchyard, looked into the church, and coming out, Philip pointed to a tombstone which from its newness among its dusky and moss-grown companions, easily struck the eye. It recorded without pious or scriptural reflection the date of the birth and death of George Hearne; the latter event had taken place close on two years ago, and we were within a week of the exact anniversary. Other tombstones near were monuments to those of the same name, and dated back for a couple of centuries and more.

"Local family," said I, and strolling on we came to our own gate in the long brick wall. It was opened from inside just as we arrived at it, and there came out a brisk middle-aged man in clergyman's dress, obviously our vicar.

He very civilly introduced himself.

"I heard that Mrs. Hearne's house had been taken, and that the tenants had come," he said, "and I ventured to leave my card."

We performed our part of the ceremony, and in answer to his inquiry professed our satisfaction with our quarters and our neighbourhood.

"That is good news," said Mr. Stephens, "I hope you will continue to enjoy your holiday. I am Cornish myself, and like all natives think there is no place like Cornwall!"

Philip pointed with his stick towards the churchyard. "We noticed that the Hearnes are people of the place," he said. Quite suddenly I found myself understanding what he had meant by the aloofness of the race. Something between reserve and suspicion came into Mr. Stephens's face.

"Yes, yes, an old family here," he said, "and large landowners. But now some remote cousin——The house, however, belongs to Mrs. Hearne for life."

He stopped, and by that reticence confirmed the impression he had made. In consequence, for there is something in the breast of the most incurious, which, when treated with reserve becomes inquisitive, Philip proceeded to ask a direct question.

"Then I take it that the George Hearne who, as I have just seen, died two years ago, was the husband of Mrs. Hearne, from whom we took the house?"

"Yes, he was buried in the churchyard," said Mr. Stephens quickly. Then, for no reason at all, he added:

"Naturally he was buried in the churchyard here."

Now my impression at that moment was that Mr. Stephens had said something he did not mean to say, and had corrected it by saying the same thing again. He went on his way, back to the vicarage, with an amiably expressed desire to do anything that was in his power for us, in the way of local information, and we went in through the gate. The post had just arrived; there was the London morning paper and a letter for Philip which cost him two perusals before he folded it up and put it into his pocket. But he made no comment, and presently, as dinner-time was near, I went up to my room. Here in this deep valley with the great westerly hill towering above us, it was already dark, and the lawn lay beneath a twilight as of deep clear water. Quite idly as I brushed my hair in front of the glass on the table in the window, of which the blinds were not yet drawn, I looked out, and saw that on the bank along which grew the pollarded limes, there was lying a ladder. It was just a shade odd that it should be there, but the oddity of it was quite accounted for by the supposition that the gardener had had business among the trees in the orchard, and had left it there, for the completion of his labours to-morrow. It was just as odd as that, and no odder, just worth a twitch of the imagination to account for it, but now completely accounted for.

I went downstairs, and passing Philip's door heard the swish of ablutions which implied he was not quite ready, and in the most loafer-like manner I strolled round the corner of the house. The kitchen window which looked on to the tennis-court was open, and there was a good smell, I remember, coming from it. And still without thought of the ladder I had just seen, I mounted the slope of grass on to the tennis-court. Just across it was the bank where the pollarded limes grew, but there was no ladder lying there. Of course, the gardener must have remembered he had left it, and had returned to remove it exactly as I came downstairs. There was nothing singular about that, and I could not imagine why the thing interested me at all. But for some inexplicable reason I found myself saying: "But I did see the ladder just now."

A bell—no telephone bell, but a welcome harbinger to a hungry man— sounded from inside the house, and I went back on to the terrace, just as Philip got downstairs. At dinner our speech rambled pleasantly over the accomplishments of to-day, and the prospects of to-morrow, and in due course we came to the consideration of Mr. Stephens. We settled that he was an aloof fellow, and then Philip said:

"I wonder why he hastened to tell us that George Hearne was buried in the churchyard, and then added that naturally he was!"

"It's the natural place to be buried in," said I.

"Quite. That's just why it was hardly worth mentioning."

I felt then, just momentarily, just vaguely, as if my mind was regarding stray pieces of a jig-saw puzzle. The fancied ringing of the telephone bell last night was one of them, this burial of George Hearne in the churchyard was another, and, even more inexplicably, the ladder I had seen under the trees was a third. Consciously I made nothing whatever out of them, and did not feel the least inclination to devote any ingenuity to so fortuitous a collection of pieces. Why shouldn't I add, for that matter, our morning's bathe, or the gorse on the hillside? But I had the sensation that, though my conscious brain was presently occupied with piquet, and was rapidly growing sleepy with the day of sun and sea, some sort of mole inside it was digging passages and connecting corridors below the soil.

Five eventless days succeeded, there were no more ladders, no more phantom telephone bells, and emphatically no more Mr. Stephens. Once or twice we met him in the village street and got from him the curtest salutation possible short of a direct cut. And yet somehow he seemed charged with information, so we lazily concluded, and he made for us a field of imaginative speculation. I remember that I constructed a highly fanciful romance, which postulated that George Hearne was not dead at all, but that Mr. Stephens had murdered some inconvenient blackmailer, whom he had buried with the rites of the church. Or—these romances always broke down under cross-examination from Philip—Mr. Stephens himself was George Hearne, who had fled from justice, and was supposed to have died. Or Mrs. Hearne was really George Hearne, and our admirable housekeeper was the real Mrs. Hearne. From such indications you may judge how the intoxication of the sun and the sea had overpowered us.

But there was one explanation of why Mr. Stephens had so hastily assured us that George Hearne was buried in the churchyard which never passed our lips. It was just because both Philip and I really believed it to be the true one, that we did not mention it. But just as if it was some fever or plague, we both knew that we were sickening with it. And then these fanciful romances stopped because we knew that the Real Thing was approaching. There had been faint glimpses of it before, like distant sheet-lightning; now the noise of it, authentic and audible, began to rumble.

There came a day of hot overclouded weather. We had bathed in the morning, and loafed in the afternoon, but Philip, after tea, had refused to come for our usual ramble, and I set out alone. That morning Mrs. Criddle had rather peremptorily told me that a room in the front of the house would prove much cooler for me, for it caught the sea-breeze, and though I objected that it would also catch the southerly sun, she had clearly made up her mind that I was to move from the bedroom overlooking the tennis-court and the pollarded limes, and there was no resisting so polite and yet determined a woman.

When I set out for my ramble after tea, the change had already been effected, and my brain nosed slowly about as I strolled sniffing for her reason, for no self-respecting brain could accept the one she gave. But in this hot drowsy air I entirely lacked nimbleness, and when I came back, the question had become a mere silly unanswerable riddle. I returned through the churchyard, and saw that in a couple of days we should arrive at the anniversary of George Hearne's death.

Philip was not on the terrace in front of the house, and I went in at the door of the hall, expecting to find him there or in the back garden. Exactly as I entered my eye told me that there he was, a black silhouette against the glass door, at the end of the hall, which was open, and led through into the back garden. He did not turn round at the sound of my entry, but took a step or two in the direction of the far door, still framed in the oblong of it. I glanced at the table, where the post lay, found letters both for me and him, and looked up again. There was no one there.

He had hastened his steps, I supposed, but simultaneously I thought how odd it was that he had not taken his letters, if he was in the hall, and that he had not turned when I entered. However, I should find him just round the corner, and with his post and mine in my hand, I went towards the far door. As I approached it I felt a sudden cold stir of air, rather unaccountable, for the day was notably sultry, and went out. He was sitting at the far end of the tennis-court.

I went up to him with his letters.

"I thought I saw you just now in the hall," I said. But I knew already that I had not seen him in the hall.

He looked up quickly.

"And have you only just come in?" he said.

"Yes; this moment. Why?"

"Because half an hour ago I went in to see if the post had come, and thought I saw you in the hall."

"And what did I do?" I asked.

"You went out on to the terrace. But I didn't find you there."

There was a short pause as he opened his letters.

"Damned interesting," he observed. "Because there's someone here who isn't you or me."

"Anything else?" I asked.

He laughed, pointing at the row of trees.

"Yes, something too silly for words," he said. "Just now I saw a piece of rope dangling from the big branch of that pollarded lime. I saw it quite distinctly. And then there wasn't any rope there at all any more than there is now."

73

Philosophers have argued about the strongest emotion known to man. Some say "love," others "hate," others "fear." I am disposed to put "curiosity" on a level, at least, with these august sensations, just mere simple inquisitiveness. Certainly at the moment it rivalled fear in my mind, and there was a hint of that.

As he spoke the parlourmaid came out into the garden with a telegram in her hand. She gave it to Philip, who without a word scribbled a line on the reply-paid form inside it, and handed it back to her.

"Dreadful nuisance," he said, "but there's no help for it. A few days ago I got a letter which made me think I might have to go up to town, and this telegram makes it certain. There's an operation possible on a patient of mine, which I hoped might have been avoided, but my locum tenens won't take the responsibility of deciding whether it is necessary or not."

He looked at his watch.

"I can catch the night train," he said, "and I ought to be able to catch the night train back from town to-morrow. I shall be back, that is to say, the day after to-morrow in the morning. There's no help for it. Ha! That telephone of yours will come in useful. I can get a taxi from Falmouth, and needn't start till after dinner."

He went into the house, and I heard him rattling and tapping at the telephone. Soon he called for Mrs. Criddle, and presently came out again.

"We're not on the telephone service," he said. "It was cut off a year ago, only they haven't removed the apparatus. But I can get a trap in the village, Mrs. Criddle says, and she's sent for it. If I start at once I shall easily be in time. Spicer's packing a bag for me, and I'll take a sandwich."

He looked sharply towards the pollarded trees.

"Yes, just there," he said. "I saw it plainly, and equally plainly I saw it not. And then there's that telephone of yours."

I told him now about the ladder I had seen below the tree where he saw the dangling rope.

"Interesting," he said, "because it's so silly and unexpected. It is really tragic that I should be called away just now, for it looks as if the—well, the matter were coming out of the darkness into a shaft of light. But I'll be back, I hope, in thirty-six hours. Meantime do observe very carefully, and whatever you do, don't make a theory. Darwin says somewhere that you can't observe without a theory, but to make a theory is a great danger to an observer. It can't help influencing your imagination; you tend to see or hear what falls in with your hypothesis. So just observe; be as mechanical as a phonograph and a photographic lens."

Presently the dog-cart arrived and I went down to the gate with him. "Whatever it is that is coming through, is coming through in bits," he said.

"You heard a telephone; I saw a rope. We both saw a figure, but not simultaneously nor in the same place. I wish I didn't have to go."

I found myself sympathising strongly with this wish, when after dinner I found myself with a solitary evening in front of me, and the pledge to "observe" binding me. It was not mainly a scientific ardour that prompted this sympathy, and the desire for independent combination, but, quite emphatically, fear of what might be coming out of the huge darkness which lies on all sides of human experience. I could no longer fail to connect together the fancied telephone bell, the rope, and the ladder, for what made the chain between them was the figure that both Philip and I had seen. Already my mind was seething with conjectural theory, but I would not let the ferment of it ascend to my surface consciousness; my business was not to aid but rather stifle my imagination.

I occupied myself, therefore, with the ordinary devices of a solitary man, sitting on the terrace, and subsequently coming into the house, for a few spots of rain began to fall. But though nothing disturbed the outward tranquillity of the evening, the quietness administered no opiate to that seething mixture of fear and curiosity that obsessed me. I heard the servants creep bedwards up the back stairs and presently I followed them. Then, forgetting for the moment that my room had been changed, I tried the handle of the door of that which I had previously occupied. It was locked.

Now here, beyond doubt, was the sign of a human agency, and at once I was determined to get into the room. The key, I could see, was not in the door, which must therefore have been locked from outside. I therefore searched the usual cache for keys along the top of the door-frame, found it, and entered.

The room was quite empty, the blinds not drawn, and after looking round it, I walked across to the window. The moon was up, and though obscured behind clouds, gave sufficient light to enable me to see objects outside with tolerable distinctness. There was the row of pollarded limes, and then with a sudden intake of my breath I saw that a foot or two below one of the boughs there was suspended something whitish and oval which oscillated as it hung there. In the dimness I could see nothing more than that, but now conjecture crashed into my conscious brain. But even as I looked it was gone again; there was nothing there but deep shadow, the trees steadfast in the windless air. Simultaneously I knew that I was not alone in the room.

I turned swiftly about, but my eyes gave no endorsement of that conviction, and yet their evidence that there was no one here except myself failed to shake it. The presence, somewhere close to me, needed no such evidence; it was self-evident though invisible, and my forehead was streaming with the abject sweat of terror. Somehow I knew that the presence was that of the figure both Philip and I had seen that evening in the hall, and, credit it or not as you will, the fact that it was invisible made it infinitely the more terrible. I knew, too, that though my eyes were blind to it, it had got into closer touch with me; I knew more of its nature now, it had had tragic and awful commerce with evil and despair. Some sort of catalepsy was on me, while it thus obsessed me; presently, minutes afterwards or perhaps mere seconds, the grip and clutch of its power was relaxed, and with shaking knees I crossed the room and went out, and again locked the door. Even as I turned the key I smiled at the futility of that. With my emergence the terror completely passed; I went across the passage leading to my room, got into bed, and was soon asleep. But I had no more need to question myself as to why Mrs. Criddle made the change. Another guest, she knew, would come to occupy it as the season arrived when George Hearne died and was buried in the churchyard.

The night passed quietly and then succeeded a day hot and still and sultry beyond belief. The very sea had lost its coolness and vitality, and I came in from my swim tired and enervated instead of refreshed. No breeze stirred; the trees stood motionless as if cast in iron, and from horizon to horizon the sky was overlaid by an ever-thickening pall of cloud. The cohorts of storm and thunder were gathering in the stillness, and all day I felt that power, other than that of these natural forces, was being stored for some imminent manifestation.

As I came near to the house the horror deepened, and after dinner I had a mind to drop into the vicarage, according to Mr. Stephens's general invitation, and get through an hour or two with other company than my own. But I delayed till it was past any reasonable time for such an informal visit, and ten o'clock still saw me on the terrace in front of the house. My nerves were all on edge, a stir or step in the house was sufficient to make me turn round in apprehension of seeing I knew not what, but presently it grew still. One lamp burned in the hall behind me; by it stood the candle which would light me to bed.

I went indoors soon after, meaning to go up to bed, then suddenly ashamed of this craven imbecility of mind, took the fancy to walk round the house for the purpose of convincing myself that all was tranquil and normal, and that my fear, that nameless indefinable load on my spirit, was but a product of this close and thundery night. The tension of the weather could not last much longer; soon the storm must break and the relief come, but it would be something to know that there was nothing more than that. Accordingly I went out again on to the terrace, traversed it and turned the corner of the house where lay the tennis lawn.

To-night the moon had not yet risen, and the darkness was such that I could barely distinguish the outline of the house, and that of the pollarded limes, but through the glass door that led from this side of the house into the hall, there shone the light of the lamp that stood there. All was absolutely quiet, and half reassured I traversed the lawn, and turned to go back. Just as I came opposite the lit door, I heard a sound very close at hand from under the deep shadow of the pollarded limes. It was as if some heavy object had fallen with a thump and rebound on the grass, and with it there came the noise of a creaking bough suddenly strained by some weight. Then interpretation came upon me with the unreasoning force of conviction, though in the blackness I could see nothing. But at the sound a horror such as I have never felt laid hold on me. It was scarcely physical at all, it came from some deep-seated region of the soul.

The heavens were rent, a stream of blinding light shot forth, and straight in front of my eyes a few yards from where I stood, I saw. The noise had been of a ladder thrown down on the grass, and from the bough of the pollarded lime, there was the figure of a man, white-faced against the blackness, oscillating and twisting on the rope that strangled him. Just that I saw before the stillness was torn to atoms by the roar of thunder, and as from a hose the rain descended. Once again, even before that first appalling riot had died, the clouds were shredded again by the lightning, and my eyes which had not moved from the place saw only the framed shadow of the trees, and their upper branches bowed by the pelting rain. All night the storm raged and bellowed making sleep impossible, and for an hour at least, between the peals of thunder, I heard the ringing of the telephone bell.

Next morning Philip returned, to whom I told exactly what is written here, but watch and observe as we might, neither of us, in the three further weeks which we spent at Polwithy, heard or saw anything that could interest the student of the occult. Pleasant lazy days succeeded each other, we bathed and rambled and played piquet of an evening, and incidentally we made friends with the vicar. He was an interesting man, full of curious lore concerning local legends and superstitions, and one night, when in our ripened acquaintanceship he had dined with us, he asked Philip directly whether either of us had experienced anything unusual during our tenancy.

Philip nodded towards me.

"My friend saw most," he said.

"May I hear it?" asked the vicar.

When I had finished, he was silent awhile.

"I think the—shall we call it explanation?—is yours by right," he said. "I will give it you if you care to hear it."

Our silence, I suppose, answered him.

"I remember meeting you two on the day after your arrival here," he said, "and you inquired about the tombstone in the churchyard erected to the memory of George Hearne. I did not want to say more of him then, for a reason that you will presently know. I told you, I recollect, perhaps rather hurriedly, that it was Mrs. Hearne's husband who was buried there. Already, I imagine, you guess that I concealed something. You may even have guessed it at the time."

He did not wait for any confirmation or repudiation of this. Sitting out on the terrace in the deep dusk, his communication was very impersonal. It was just a narrating voice, without identity, an anonymous chronicle.

"George Hearne succeeded to the property here, which is considerable, only two years before his death. He was married shortly after he succeeded. According to any decent standard, his life both before and after his marriage was vile. I think—God forgive me if I wrong him—he made evil his good; he liked evil for its own sake. But out of the middle of the mire of his own soul there sprang a flower: he was devoted to his wife. And he was capable of shame.

"A fortnight before his—his death, she got to know what his life was like, and what he was in himself. I need not tell you what was the particular disclosure that came to her knowledge; it is sufficient to say that it was revolting. She was here at the time; he was coming down from London that night. When he arrived he found a note from her saying that she had left him and could never come back. She told him that he must give her opportunity for her to divorce him, and threatened him with exposure if he did not.

"He and I had been friends, and that night he came to me with her letter, acknowledged the justice of it, but asked me to intervene. He said that the only thing that could save him from utter damnation was she, and I believe that there he spoke sincerely. But, speaking as a clergyman, I should not have called him penitent. He did not hate his sin, but only the consequences of it. But it seemed to me that if she came back to him, he might have a chance, and next day I went to her. Nothing that I could say moved her one atom, and after a fruitless day I came back, and told him of the uselessness of my mission.

"Now, according to my view, no man who deliberately prefers evil to good, just for the sake of wickedness, is sane, and this refusal of hers to have anything more to do with him, I fully believe upset the unstable balance of his soul altogether. There was just his devotion to her which might conceivably have restored it, but she refused—and I can quite understand her refusal—to come near him. If you knew what I know, you could not blame her. But the effect of it on him was portentous and disastrous, and three days afterwards I wrote to her again, saying quite simply that the damnation of his soul would be on her head unless, leaving her personal feelings altogether out of the question, she came back. She got that letter the next evening, and already it was too late.

"That afternoon, two years ago, on the 15th of August, there was washed up in the harbour here a dead body, and that night George Hearne took a ladder from the fruit-wall in the kitchen garden and hanged himself. He climbed into one of the pollarded limes, tied the rope to a bough, and made a slip-knot at the other end of it. Then he kicked the ladder away.

"Mrs. Hearne meantime had received my letter. For a couple of hours she wrestled with her own repugnance and then decided to come to him. She rang him up on the telephone, but the housekeeper here, Mrs. Criddle, could only tell her that he had gone out after dinner. She continued ringing him up for a couple of hours, but there was always the same reply.

"Eventually she decided to waste no more time, and motored over from her mother's house where she was staying at the north end of the county. By then the moon had risen, and looking out from his bedroom window she saw him."

He paused.

"There was an inquest," he said, "and I could truthfully testify that I believed him to be insane. The verdict of suicide during temporary insanity was brought in, and he was buried in the churchyard. The rope was burned, and the ladder was burned."

The parlourmaid brought out drinks, and we sat in silence till she had gone again.

"And what about the telephone my friend heard?" asked Philip.

He thought a moment.

"Don't you think that great emotion like that of Mrs. Hearne's may make some sort of record," he asked, "so that if the needle of a sensitive temperament comes in contact with it, a reproduction takes place? And it is the same perhaps about that poor fellow who hanged himself. One can hardly believe that his spirit is bound to visit and revisit the scene of his follies and his crimes year by year."

"Year by year?" I asked.

"Apparently. I saw him myself last year, Mrs. Criddle did also."

He got up.

"How can one tell?" he said. "Expiation, perhaps. Who knows?"

VIII

HOME, SWEET HOME

It was pleasant to get out of the baked train into an atmosphere that tingled with the subtle vitality of the sea, and though nothing could be duller than the general prospect of flat fields and dusty hedgerows, and the long white road that lay straight as a ruled line between them, I surmised that when it had climbed that long upward slope, there would be a new horizon altogether, grey and liquid. Eyethorpe Junction was the name of the station, and though that appeared a strange misnomer, for nothing seemed to join anything, I presently perceived a weedy, derelict branch line, and a loquacious porter explained that the line to Eyethorpe had long been untraversed by railway traffic. There had once been high hopes that it would develop into a popular watering-place. But the public had preferred its established favourites.

The affairs that led to my disembarkation on this broiling August day at a jointless junction had been conducted in my sister Margery's most characteristic style. Her husband, Walter Mostyn, the eminent nerve specialist, had been threatened during July with a breakdown owing to overstrain in his work, and, in obedience to the ironical ordinance of "Physician, heal thyself," had prescribed for himself a complete rest. His idea of resting his mind was not, as is the usual practice of those on holiday, to overtire his body, but to get away to some place where there was no temptation to do anything of the kind. There must be no golf-links, or he would want to play golf, and he would prefer his retreat to be by the sea, because the very fact of being in a boat at all made him feel seasick, and he hated bathing. A rest-cure in a nursing-home would be horrible to him, and he thought that if Margery could find some deadly seaside resort, where there was nothing that could tempt him into activity of mind or body, that would do just as well. He wanted to be a beast of the field, and recover his nervous force by sheer vegetation.

Margery, with these instructions to guide her, had thereupon set off, and scoured the coasts of Kent and Sussex, discovering on the second day of her wild career this amazing and unique Eyethorpe. There was a house there to let, which she at once saw was just what she was looking for, and with that most unfeminine instinct of hers of knowing that she had got what she wanted, and not making any further search, she went straight to the house-agent at Hastings and took "The Firs" for a month as from to-morrow. She drove back to London that evening, informed Walter what she had done, sent down her servants next morning, and took down her husband the same evening. A fortnight later she wrote to me that the cure was progressing splendidly, and that he, emerging from his languor, was getting rather cross and argumentative, which she took to be the sign of returning vitality. He was excessively bored with her, and wanted some man in the house, and had grudgingly said that I would "do." So would I come soon for a couple of weeks? In fact, I must, and she would expect me on Thursday. It was Thursday now, and, in consequence, I was driving up the straight, white road from Eyethorpe Junction.

We topped the rise, and there, as I had expected, was a new horizon. The sea sprang up to eye-level, the ground declined steeply over a stretch of open downland dotted with furze bushes to a line of low cliffs that fringed the shore. Along the edge of these was a huddle of red-roofed cottages, among which rose a conspicuous church-tower, and presently we jolted over the level-crossing of the line from Eyethorpe Junction, which the public had scorned. On the left was a small abandoned station with weed-grown platform, and a board, much defaced by the weather, bearing the inscription "Eyethorpe and Coltham." The name Coltham stirred some remote vibration in my mind; I felt that I had heard the name before, but could not recall the reason for its faint familiarity. The road forked, the left-hand branch of it leading up the village street; the other, which we took, had a signpost with the information that Coltham was one mile distant. We traversed, I should have guessed, two or three furlongs, and there, close at hand, separated from the highway by a field, through which led a grass-grown drive, stood a big mellow-walled farmhouse. A clump of rather fine Scotch firs at one end of it was sufficient indication of its identity.

I was taken into and through a broad passage (you might call it a hall) which intersected the house, and from which a dignified staircase led to the upper storey. At its further end a glass-paned door opened into the garden. But there was no one here, and the servant supposed that they had gone strolling, perhaps down to the beach. The afternoon was still very hot, and, deciding to wait for them rather than vaguely pursue, I admired the luck that had attended Margery's search for a tranquil sanatorium. Not a house was visible; the clean emptiness of the downland was laid like a broad green riband east and west, and in front, through a V-shaped gap, gleamed the sea. A one-storied wing, evidently a later addition, sprouted from the west end of the house; this cast just now a very welcome shade over the square space, laid with old paving-stones, where long, low chairs and the tea-table stood. The added wing, it is scarcely necessary to mention, was of far more antique design than the house, and, looking in through its open door which gave on to this flagged space, I found a very big, pleasant room, with rafters in the ceiling, and small diamond-shaped panes in the mullioned windows. The oak floor was bare but for a few rugs, and at the far end, near an open fireplace, stood a grand piano. The lid was open, and I read there, to my great surprise, the world-famous name of Barenstein. That, too, was just like Margery, to take a remote farmhouse and find a Barenstein grand waiting for her very gifted fingers, and this fine spacious room. How cool it was in here, too— more than cool, it was positively cold; and at that moment, hearing familiar voices outside, I stepped out again on to the paved space from which I had entered.

Certainly Walter did not look as if a fortnight ago he had been on the edge of nervous breakdown. His face was bronzed and ruddy, he strode along with a firm step, and was talking in that loud, confident voice that had so often brought comfort to sufferers.

"But I tell you, darling," he was saying, "that it isn't that our senses occasionally deceive us, they habitually deceive us. Ah! there he is. Welcome, my dear Ted. You have come to a place beyond the limits of the civilised world, and it has done me a world of good already. Distractions, things that interest us are what starves the nerves. Boredom, there's the panacea for nerves. I've never been so bored in my life, and I'm a new man."

Margery laughed.

"I wonder how often you've told your patients exactly the opposite," she said. "(Ted, there's a magnificent Barenstein here; did you ever know such luck?) But isn't it so, Walter? You always say that there's hope even for people who take an interest in postage-stamps. Never mind. You hate being consistent, and I won't press it. What about the senses habitually deceiving us?"

"Obvious. Your eyes, for instance. If you see a house half a mile off, your eyes tell you it is about a quarter of an inch in height. If another train passes you as yours is standing in a station, they will tell you that you are moving in the opposite direction. Smell and taste are the same; if you shut your eyes you have no idea whether your cigarette is alight. Your sense of warmth and cold too; if you put your hand on a piece of very cold metal, it gives you the sensation of burning. I'm just as bad as you, perhaps worse, for my senses tell me that that room in there is bitterly cold to-day, but the thermometer says it is 65 degrees. I was suffering from some subjective disturbance, that was all, and my imbecile senses told me it was cold. There was the thermometer saying it was warm. The senses, as I tell you, are habitually deceptive. Liars!"

There was all his usual vehemence in this, and, so I thought, a little more. He was clearly upset at this divergence of view between his senses and the thermometer.

"But I'm on the side of your senses," I said. "I went in there just now, and I swear it was more than chilly."

He threw a quick glance over to Margery before he answered.

"More liars then!" he said. "Another instance of the deceptiveness of the senses."

He said this with the air of bringing the discussion to an end; our talk became desultory and trivial, and before long Margery closed it by saying that, whatever anybody else did, she intended to have a dip in the sea before dinner. Presently she appeared again, with sandals and a dressing-gown over her bathing-suit, for there was but this strip of empty downland between the garden and the steep short descent on the beach. She insisted on my accompanying her as far as that V-shaped gap, and her very casual manner made me sure that she had some communication to make. It came as soon as we were out of earshot.

"Walter's ever so much better, as you can see for yourself," she said, "and till to-day he has been lying fallow with the most excellent results. But now that awful activity of his mind has begun to work again, and twenty times since lunch he has alluded to that strange feeling of chill in the big room in the wing. He keeps on saying that it's subjective, but you and I know him, and that means he thinks there's something queer about it. And you felt it, too, apparently."

"I thought I did, but then I had just come into it from the broiling air outside. But hadn't he felt it before?"

"No, for the simple reason that he hadn't been into the room before," said she. "When we came here, and, indeed, till this morning, it was locked and shuttered. The gardener, who has been caretaker here, told me that the owner had stored things in it, and that it was to be left closed. Till this morning Walter did not seem to mind whether it was shut or open, but to-day he told the gardener that it was all nonsense to keep the biggest room in the house shut up, and demanded the key. Denton, that's his name, talked about disobeying his owner, but Walter insisted, and he produced the key. There was nothing stored there, and I drove over to the house-agent's at Hastings this morning to ask if there was any such order. None at all. What does it mean?"

"Nothing," said I, "except that Denton was a lazy brute, and didn't want the bother of airing and dusting the room before you came, and of putting it to rights again after you'd gone. Perhaps also the owner didn't want to prohibit your playing the great Barenstein, but hoped you wouldn't. Also this accounts for the fact that Walter and I found the room very chilly after it had been shut up for so long. When was the house last occupied, by the way?"

"I don't know. It had been unlet for some time, so the agent told me, and I didn't care in the least about its history provided I got it for Walter now."

Her jolly brown eyes made a complete circuit round my head, instead of looking at me straight when she answered.

"Don't be so foolish, Margery," I said, "but look straight at me. You told me just now that Walter thought there was something queer about the room. What do you think?"

Her eyes rested on mine.

"I think there's something queer about the house," she said. "I find myself looking up suddenly from a book or a paper to see who is in the room. And I think Walter does the same. But he—he thinks he hears something, and then finds he hasn't, just as I think I see something, and find I haven't. I cock an eye, he cocks an ear. But don't say a word to him. He hates the idea of anything you can't account for by the ordinary functions of the senses, which, he says, habitually deceive you. But since that room was opened, he's been arguing with himself."

"Oh, put the stopper in," said I. "Do you remember the gurgle of the hot-water pipes in the nursery thirty years ago, and how you knew it was the groan of a murdered woman? You frightened me out of my wits then, but I'm too old to be frightened now. You haven't seen anything, and he hasn't heard anything; eye hath not seen nor ear heard. Don't imagine things; half the trouble in the world comes from imagining. Have a nice bathe, and wash it all off."

For a moment, as she looked at me, I saw somewhere behind her eyes a sense of uneasiness, but it vanished.

"I shan't wash off my gladness that you've joined us," she said, and ran off down the steep little path to the beach.

I strolled back through the garden thinking how unlike Margery it was to be within the grip of vague apprehension like this, or to imagine that there was anything "queer" about the house, for in spite of the famous episode of the gurgling pipes, she was singularly free from imagined alarms. Even more unusual, if she was right about him, was it that Walter should be affected in the same sort of way. Margery certainly showed her good sense in demanding that her odd apprehensions should be kept apart from his, and not be given the meeting-ground of discussion. But she had noticed, or imagined, his, and I was soon to learn that he was not blind to hers.

Walter had gone up to his room when I got back, and I went into the lately opened sitting-room, where I found that my books and papers had been disposed on a big table, which was thus clearly consecrated to my use. I was engaged on a memoir which it interested me to write, though I had grave doubts about its interesting anybody else to read. The piano stood a little beyond my table, with the keyboard towards me; between it and me, on my left, was the open window looking on to the garden. The room still seemed chilly, but I speedily forgot that and, indeed, everything else but my delightful task.

How long I had been at work I had no idea, when suddenly—even as I turned a page to carry on the note I had begun—I became vividly aware of my surroundings again and knew with absolute conviction that I was not alone. I glanced up and saw that there was a man outside the window looking at the piano. For a second or two he gazed fixedly at it, and then, turning his head, perceived me at my table. He had not, I imagined, observed that there was anyone here, for he touched his hat, and would have gone away, but I called to him.

"Do you want anything?" I asked. "Denton, is it?"

"Yes, sir. I—I was only just looking to see if the room was all right," and immediately he withdrew. But, oddly enough, I felt that it was not Denton's presence at the window that gave me the sense that there was someone here; it had nothing to do with Denton. And why, I asked myself, as the man walked briskly off, why on earth should Denton look in to see if the room was all right? It was the piano that riveted him; did he want to be sure that all was well with the piano?

I tried to attach myself to my work again, but the connection would no longer hold. There was still that sense of some presence in the room, which came between me and my page. Time and again I held my mind down to its task, but it slipped away, and presently at its bidding my eyes left the paper and scrutinised the room. Certainly there was nothing behind me, nor at my side, but I found myself—was it Denton's example which had infected me?—looking at the piano, as if what I sought was invisibly there. Its japanned case, darkly, like black glass, reflected my table, the white keys gleamed in their ebony setting. And then I saw that some of them were moving—a group, three or four at a time, and now a succession of single notes sank and recovered as if under the pressure of fingers.

I cannot hope to describe the curiosity and the dismay with which this filled my mind. I gazed fascinated at this inexplicable movement, but at the same time my mind cried out in horror at the invisible cause of it. Then, as suddenly as it had begun, this fantastic spectacle ceased, but the presence was still there. Then from outside there came the sound of steps. Walter entered.

"Margery here?" he asked. "No? Was it you playing, then?"

"Deceptive senses," I said. "I haven't touched the piano."

He looked at me a moment, puzzled.

"But I would swear I heard the piano," he said.

Instantly I made up my mind not to tell Walter what I had seen, and already, so fantastic was it, I was beginning to doubt if I had seen anything. Yet deep in my mind remained that intense curiosity, and deeper yet some unreasoning terror.

The evening passed quite normally; Walter bewailed the hideous necessity of going in to Hastings next day to have his hair cut, and the even darker fate of having the Vicar of Eyethorpe to dinner.

It was still early when we went up to bed and, conscious of an overwhelming somnolence, I instantly fell asleep. I woke, staring wide awake, with the answer to the question which had slightly worried me yesterday, as to why the name of the neighbouring Coltham was remotely familiar to me, clear in my mind. There had occurred there, about a year before, a very brutal murder, which still remained among the unsolved mysteries of criminal history. An elderly spinster lady, living with her spinster sister at some house there, had been found strangled on the floor of her sitting-room. It was supposed that robbery was the motive for the crime, but the murderer seemed to have heard some stir in the house, and left a cashbox containing thirty or forty pounds in the drawer he had just opened. I could remember no further details, but I thought I would stroll over to Coltham next morning and, with that appetite for the horrible which lurks in us all, find out which the house was.

The two went off to Hastings next morning and, in pursuance of my plan, I strolled up the road to Coltham. It was a melancholy little bunch of cottages perched on the edge of the downs, and I had just decided that a rather stricken-looking house, with a board up to say it was to let, was a suitable site for the murder, when I saw Denton coming down the little street.

"Which was the house where that murder took place last year, Denton?" I asked him.

He stared at me a moment, and I saw his throat-apple jerk up and down. Then he pointed to the house I had picked out.

"That was the one, sir," he said.

"And what was the name of the old lady?" I asked.

"Miss Ellershaw," said he, and rather abruptly, much in the manner in which he had retreated from the window last night, he turned and left me. Rather pleased with myself for my perspicacity I strolled homewards again.

Margery and Walter, he shorn and self-respecting again, came back about one o'clock, and Margery announced her determination of writing overdue letters till the really intolerable heat of the day had declined.

"Hopeless arrears," she said, "bills and bills, and the rent of the house for the next fortnight, which ought to have been paid two days ago. But I'll send it straight to our landlord—or is it landlady?—instead of the agent; that will save a day."

The clear burning of the sun had given place to an extreme sultriness; the sky was overcast with clouds which all afternoon thickened to a still density portending thunder. Margery retired to the piano-room to perform her overdues, Walter fell asleep and, leaving him on the paved space, I joined Margery for coolness. She jumped up as I entered.

"I was dying to be interrupted," she said, "because I long to see what's in that cupboard by the piano. I've muddled up your papers, Ted, I'm afraid. Unmuddle them again while I have an interval."

She had, indeed, muddled my papers up. Half-finished letters, and addressed envelopes, and bills were mixed up with my notes. As I disentangled them, I came across a cheque she had drawn. It was made out to Miss Ellershaw. There was also a half-sheet on which Mrs. Mostyn "much regretted not having sent cheque for a fortnight's rent sooner."... So Miss Ellershaw was owner of "The Firs," and two Miss Ellershaws, one of whom had been murdered, lived together. Had they lived in that house at Coltham, where Denton had told me the murder was committed, or had they...?

Margery interrupted these rather disquieting thoughts.

"What a disappointment!" she said. "Empty cupboard, all but one leaf of a book of English songs, and that's 'Home, Sweet Home!' You may laugh at it, but it's a wonderful melody. I must just play it, and then I shall get on with my jobs."

The window close to which I sat commanded a view of the garden. Out of it, I could see Denton plucking sweet peas. As the notes of the old-fashioned tune streamed out through the open window, I saw him drop his basket and stop his ears. Simultaneously, I knew that there was some presence, here in the room, not Margery's nor mine.

She played two lines and stopped. She turned round and faced me.

"What is there here?" she said. "And what——?"

Walter, whom I had left asleep, looked in at the door.

"Ah, it's you playing," he said. "That's all right."

By strange interweavings of emotion, that common consciousness between us all of the presence of something that came not from among the humming wheels of life but from the grey mists that encompassed it, grew thicker in texture. There was some presence in the room—not mine, nor Margery's, nor Walter's—here now, though invisible, and somehow gathering strength from our recognition of its existence. In our different ways we all contributed to it in that moment of absolute and appalling silence.

Some sort of babble broke it. I babbled of the disorder of my papers, Margery babbled apology and promised to put them straight, if she might be allowed to deal with them. Some sort of crisis passed. I can explain it no better than that.

As evening drew on the clouds gathered even more thickly. The sea was leaden, the air dead, and when, about half-past ten that night, Mr. Bird, who had proved himself a charming guest, said good night, and I went with him to the door, we looked out on to a pit of impenetrable darkness. I saw the opportunity I wanted, and assuring him that I should really like a stroll to get such air as there was, insisted on fetching a lantern and lighting him back as far as the village. I then went straight to the point.

"There was a fearful tragedy in Coltham last year," I said. "Denton pointed me out the house where the murder was committed."

Mr. Bird stopped dead.

"Denton pointed you out the house?" he asked.

"Yes, but perhaps he was wrong," said I. "In fact, Mr. Bird, I should be very much obliged to you if you would tell me whether I am not right in thinking that the scene of the tragedy was 'The Firs.' My sister and brother-in-law know nothing about it, and I hope they won't. But I learned accidentally to-day that she pays the rent to Miss Ellershaw, which I think is the name. And I hazard the guess that the precise scene was the room outside which we sat to-night."

He did not reply for a moment.

"I can't deny what you suggest," he said, "and my mere refusal to reply would do no good. You are quite right. Denton's telling you, by the way, that the scene was in the village, itself, is quite intelligible, for Miss Ellershaw, who does not intend to live in the house again, wants to let it, and if it was known that the murder took place there, it would be prejudicial, Denton knows that. And in turn I want to ask you something. Why do you guess that particular room?"

I hesitated as to whether I should tell him about the crop of strange impressions which were growing up round it, but decided not to.

"There are queer things," I said. "My sister was told, for instance, that there were orders that the room should not be used. Denton told her that."

"I can understand that, too," he said. "The room has terrible memories for those who were in the house at the time. Any more queer things?"

"None that I can think of at present," I said. "But I will wish you good night here, as the rest of your way is clear."

I retraced my steps, and found that Walter and Margery had both gone upstairs. There was a lamp still burning on the paved space where we had sat after dinner, and I went out there, disinclined to go to bed, with my nerves all strung up by the stimulus of the approaching storm. All feeling of fear about what was creeping out into the light concerning this room, and what might, I felt, suddenly burst forth with some blaze of revelation, was gone, and I was conscious only of intense curiosity, as I summed up in my mind what I believed, owing to these strange hints and signals out of the mists, had actually taken place. I figured Miss Ellershaw as having been sitting at the piano when the strangling cord was slipped round her neck; I figured her as having been playing "Home, Sweet Home"; I figured Denton as having heard her. Then there would have been silence, but for some few gasps, some quivering convulsions, like the shaking of leaves in a tree, and then the discovery, perhaps by Denton, of the crime which was still unexplained. Certainly that afternoon, the fragment of the tune which Margery had played, gave him a sudden shock of horror....

The night was absolutely still; neither from inside the house nor from outside came the slightest stir of life, and the silence rang in my ears. And then from the room close at hand I heard, faint but distinct, the tinkle of the piano. A couple of bars of the familiar tune were played, and some voice, thin and quavering, began to sing the air. Curiosity, violent and irresistible, drowned all other feeling in my mind, and taking up the lamp, I opened the door of the room and entered. It burned brightly, and by its light, which gleamed on the keys of the piano, I could see that the room was empty. But the tune went on, softly played and faintly sung, and looking more closely at the piano, I saw that once more the keys were moving. At that the sense of fear which till then had lain coiled and quiet in my mind, began to stir. But I felt absolutely powerless to go; fear, now in swift invasion of my mind, held me where I was.

Something began to form in the air by the piano, a mist, a greyness. Then in a second it solidified, and there sat with her back to me the figure of a little white-haired woman. Then the singing stopped, her arms shot up with quivering, clutching fingers; she struggled, she turned, and I saw her face, swollen and purple, with gasping mouth and protruding eyes. Her head lolled and nodded; her body swayed backwards and forwards, and she slid off the music-stool to the ground. At that moment a blaze of light poured through the unsheltered windows, and I saw pressed against the pane, and seemingly quite unaware of my presence, Denton's white and staring countenance. His eyes were fixed on the piano. Simultaneously with the light came an appalling crack of thunder. The storm had burst.

For that moment Denton and I faced each other; the next he had gone, and I heard his feet running down the garden path. I had seen enough, too, and with my mind submerged in terror I stumbled from the room. As I paused for a moment outside, another flash flooded the gross darkness, and I saw him scudding across the down to the white edge of the cliffs. Then down came the rain, solid and hissing, my lamp was extinguished, and by the flare of the lightning, standing still between the flashes, I groped my way up to bed.

All night the prodigious storm streamed and rattled, but about dawn, as I lay still sleepless, and quaking with the prodigy of horror I had looked upon, it passed away, and I dozed and then slept deeply, and woke to find the morning tranquil and fresh and sunny. All the intolerable depression of the day before, not physical alone, seemed to me to have vanished, the house was wholesome as the breeze from the sea, and so, too, when, not without making a strong call on my courage, I entered it, I found the room where last night I had witnessed that ghastly pageantry. In no way could I account for that inward conviction, even less could I question it; all I knew was that some tragic stain had passed from it.

I was down before either of the others, and strolling through the garden as I waited for them, I saw advancing along the paved walk the figure of the Vicar.

"A very dreadful thing has happened," he said. "Denton's body was found half an hour ago by some fishermen at the foot of the cliff down there. His head was smashed in; he must have fallen sheer on to the rocks."

Now the reader may put any interpretation he pleases on the events which I have here briefly recorded, and on certain facts which may or may not seem to him to be connected with them, namely, that Miss Ellershaw, the elder of the two sisters who lived together at "The Firs," was found strangled on the floor by the piano in the room which juts out into the garden; that her sister not many minutes before her body was found had heard her singing "Home, Sweet Home" to her own accompaniment, and that the author of the murder had never been found. It is a fact also that late on the night of which I have been speaking, I saw Denton looking in through the window of that room, and shortly afterwards running across the strip of downland towards the cliff, at the bottom of which next morning his body was found.

But beyond that point we deal not with material facts, but with impressions. Three separate people fancied that there was something strange about the room; one of them found herself expecting to see some unaccountable appearance; one of them thought there was a peculiar chill in the room, and also that he heard the piano being played when nobody had touched it; the third, as I have related, believed that he both saw and heard things in that room which he cannot explain. Whether Denton shared that experience we cannot tell, nor can we tell for certain whether it was a pure accident that he fell over the cliff, or whether he had seen and heard something which drove him to make an end of himself.

It remains only to add that Walter and Margery agreed that some strange sense, which they had both felt as of an unexplained presence in that room, had passed away from it during the night on which Denton met his death. Walter was inclined to attribute our original impressions to some purely subjective disturbance of the nerves caused by the approach of that great storm. Not then, but later when thoroughly restored, he had gone back to his work I told him and Margery what I had seen that night and what, perhaps, Denton had seen.

IX

"AND NO BIRD SINGS"

The red chimneys of the house for which I was bound were visible from just outside the station at which I had alighted, and, so the chauffeur told me, the distance was not more than a mile's walk if I took the path across the fields. It ran straight till it came to the edge of that wood yonder, which belonged to my host, and above which his chimneys were visible. I should find a gate in the paling of this wood, and a track traversing it, which debouched close to his garden. So, in this adorable afternoon of early May, it seemed a waste of time to do other than walk through meadows and woods, and I set off on foot, while the motor carried my traps.

It was one of those golden days which every now and again leak out of Paradise and drip to earth. Spring had been late in coming, but now it was here with a burst, and the whole world was boiling with the sap of life. Never have I seen such a wealth of spring flowers, or such vividness of green, or heard such melodious business among the birds in the hedgerows; this walk through the meadows was a jubilee of festal ecstasy. And best of all, so I promised myself, would be the passage through the wood newly fledged with milky green that lay just ahead. There was the gate, just facing me, and I passed through it into the dappled lights and shadows of the grass-grown track.

Coming out of the brilliant sunshine was like entering a dim tunnel; one had the sense of being suddenly withdrawn from the brightness of the spring into some subaqueous cavern. The tree-tops formed a green roof overhead, excluding the light to a remarkable degree; I moved in a world of shifting obscurity. Presently, as the trees grew more scattered, their place was taken by a thick growth of hazels, which met over the path, and then, the ground sloping downwards, I came upon an open clearing, covered with bracken and heather, and studded with birches. But though now I walked once more beneath the luminous sky, with the sunlight pouring down, it seemed to have lost its effulgence. The brightness—was it some odd optical illusion?—was veiled as if it came through crêpe. Yet there was the sun still well above the tree-tops in an unclouded heaven, but for all that the light was that of a stormy winter's day, without warmth or brilliance. It was oddly silent, too; I had thought that the bushes and trees would be ringing with the song of mating-birds, but listening, I could hear no note of any sort, neither the fluting of thrush or blackbird, nor the cheerful whirr of the chaffinch, nor the cooing wood-pigeon, nor the strident clamour of the jay. I paused to verify

90

this odd silence; there was no doubt about it. It was rather eerie, rather uncanny, but I supposed the birds knew their own business best, and if they were too busy to sing it was their affair.

As I went on it struck me also that since entering the wood I had not seen a bird of any kind; and now, as I crossed the clearing, I kept my eyes alert for them, but fruitlessly, and soon I entered the further belt of thick trees which surrounded it. Most of them I noticed were beeches, growing very close to each other, and the ground beneath them was bare but for the carpet of fallen leaves, and a few thin bramble-bushes. In this curious dimness and thickness of the trees, it was impossible to see far to right or left of the path, and now, for the first time since I had left the open, I heard some sound of life. There came the rustle of leaves from not far away, and I thought to myself that a rabbit, anyhow, was moving. But somehow it lacked the staccato patter of a small animal; there was a certain stealthy heaviness about it, as if something much larger were stealing along and desirous of not being heard. I paused again to see what might emerge, but instantly the sound ceased. Simultaneously I was conscious of some faint but very foul odour reaching me, a smell choking and corrupt, yet somehow pungent, more like the odour of something alive rather than rotting. It was peculiarly sickening, and not wanting to get any closer to its source I went on my way.

Before long I came to the edge of the wood; straight in front of me was a strip of meadow-land, and beyond an iron gate between two brick walls, through which I had a glimpse of lawn and flower-beds. To the left stood the house, and over house and garden there poured the amazing brightness of the declining afternoon.

Hugh Granger and his wife were sitting out on the lawn, with the usual pack of assorted dogs: a Welsh collie, a yellow retriever, a fox-terrier, and a Pekinese. Their protest at my intrusion gave way to the welcome of recognition, and I was admitted into the circle. There was much to say, for I had been out of England for the last three months, during which time Hugh had settled into this little estate left him by a recluse uncle, and he and Daisy had been busy during the Easter vacation with getting into the house. Certainly it was a most attractive legacy; the house, through which I was presently taken, was a delightful little Queen Anne manor, and its situation on the edge of this heather-clad Surrey ridge quite superb. We had tea in a small panelled parlour overlooking the garden, and soon the wider topics narrowed down to those of the day and the hour. I had walked, had I, asked Daisy, from the station: did I go through the wood, or follow the path outside it?

The question she thus put to me was given trivially enough; there was no hint in her voice that it mattered a straw to her which way I had come. But it was quite clearly borne in upon me that not only she but Hugh also listened intently for my reply. He had just lit a match for his cigarette, but held it unapplied till he heard my answer. Yes, I had gone through the wood; but now, though I had received some odd impressions in the wood, it seemed quite ridiculous to mention what they were. I could not soberly say that the sunshine there was of very poor quality, and that at one point in my traverse I had smelt a most iniquitous odour. I had walked through the wood; that was all I had to tell them.

I had known both my host and hostess for a tale of many years, and now, when I felt that there was nothing except purely fanciful stuff that I could volunteer about my experiences there, I noticed that they exchanged a swift glance, and could easily interpret it. Each of them signalled to the other an expression of relief; they told each other (so I construed their glance) that I, at any rate, had found nothing unusual in the wood, and they were pleased at that. But then, before any real pause had succeeded to my answer that I had gone through the wood, I remembered that strange absence of bird-song and birds, and as that seemed an innocuous observation in natural history, I thought I might as well mention it.

"One odd thing struck me," I began (and instantly I saw the attention of both riveted again), "I didn't see a single bird or hear one from the time I entered the wood to when I left it."

Hugh lit his cigarette.

"I've noticed that too," he said, "and it's rather puzzling. The wood is certainly a bit of primeval forest, and one would have thought that hosts of birds would have nested in it from time immemorial. But, like you, I've never heard or seen one in it. And I've never seen a rabbit there either."

"I thought I heard one this afternoon," said I. "Something was moving in the fallen beech leaves."

"Did you see it?" he asked.

I recollected that I had decided that the noise was not quite the patter of a rabbit.

"No, I didn't see it," I said, "and perhaps it wasn't one. It sounded, I remember, more like something larger."

Once again and unmistakably a glance passed between Hugh and his wife, and she rose.

"I must be off," she said. "Post goes out at seven, and I lazed all morning. What are you two going to do?"

"Something out of doors, please," said I. "I want to see the domain."

Hugh and I accordingly strolled out again with the cohort of dogs. The domain was certainly very charming; a small lake lay beyond the garden, with a reed bed vocal with warblers, and a tufted margin into which coots and moorhens scudded at our approach. Rising from the end of that was a high heathery knoll full of rabbit holes, which the dogs nosed at with joyful expectations, and there we sat for a while overlooking the wood which covered the rest of the estate. Even now in the blaze of the sun near to its setting, it seemed to be in shadow, though like the rest of the view it should have basked in brilliance, for not a cloud flecked the sky and the level rays enveloped the world in a crimson splendour. But the wood was grey and darkling. Hugh, also, I was aware, had been looking at it, and now, with an air of breaking into a disagreeable topic, he turned to me.

"Tell me," he said, "does anything strike you about that wood?"

"Yes: it seems to lie in shadow."

He frowned.

"But it can't, you know," he said. "Where does the shadow come from? Not from outside, for sky and land are on fire."

"From inside, then?" I asked

He was silent a moment.

"There's something queer about it," he said at length. "There's something there, and I don't know what it is. Daisy feels it too; she won't ever go into the wood, and it appears that birds won't either. Is it just the fact that, for some unexplained reason, there are no birds in it that has set all our imaginations at work?"

I jumped up.

"Oh, it's all rubbish," I said. "Let's go through it now and find a bird. I bet you I find a bird."

"Sixpence for every bird you see," said Hugh.

We went down the hillside and walked round the wood till we came to the gate where I had entered that afternoon. I held it open after I had gone in for the dogs to follow. But there they stood, a yard or so away, and none of them moved.

"Come on, dogs," I said, and Fifi, the fox-terrier, came a step nearer and then with a little whine retreated again.

"They always do that," said Hugh, "not one of them will set foot inside the wood. Look!"

He whistled and called, he cajoled and scolded, but it was no use. There the dogs remained, with little apologetic grins and signallings of tails, but quite determined not to come.

"But why?" I asked.

"Same reason as the birds, I suppose, whatever that happens to be. There's Fifi, for instance, the sweetest-tempered little lady; once I tried to pick her up and carry her in, and she snapped at me. They'll have nothing to do with the wood; they'll trot round outside it and go home."

We left them there, and in the sunset light which was now beginning to fade began the passage. Usually the sense of eeriness disappears if one has a companion, but now to me, even with Hugh walking by my side, the place seemed even more uncanny than it had done that afternoon, and a sense of intolerable uneasiness, that grew into a sort of waking nightmare, obsessed me. I had thought before that the silence and loneliness of it had played tricks with my nerves; but with Hugh here it could not be that, and indeed I felt that it was not any such notion that lay at the root of this fear, but rather the conviction that there was some presence lurking there, invisible as yet, but permeating the gathered gloom. I could not form the slighted idea of what it might be, or whether it was material or ghostly; all I could diagnose of it from my own sensations was that it was evil and antique.

As we came to the open ground in the middle of the wood, Hugh stopped, and though the evening was cool I noticed that he mopped his forehead.

"Pretty nasty," he said. "No wonder the dogs don't like it. How do you feel about it?"

Before I could answer, he shot out his hand, pointing to the belt of trees that lay beyond.

"What's that?" he said in a whisper.

I followed his finger, and for one half-second thought I saw against the black of the wood some vague flicker, grey or faintly luminous. It waved as if it had been the head and forepart of some huge snake rearing itself, but it instantly disappeared, and my glimpse had been so momentary that I could not trust my impression.

"It's gone," said Hugh, still looking in the direction he had pointed; and as we stood there, I heard again what I had heard that afternoon, a rustle among the fallen beech-leaves. But there was no wind nor breath of breeze astir.

He turned to me.

"What on earth was it?" he said. "It looked like some enormous slug standing up. Did you see it?"

"I'm not sure whether I did or not," I said. "I think I just caught sight of what you saw."

"But what was it?" he said again. "Was it a real material creature, or was it——"

"Something ghostly, do you mean?" I asked.

"Something half-way between the two," he said. "I'll tell you what I mean afterwards, when we've got out of this place."

The thing, whatever it was, had vanished among the trees to the left of where our path lay, and in silence we walked across the open till we came to where it entered tunnel-like among the trees. Frankly I hated and feared the thought of plunging into that darkness with the knowledge that not so far off there was something the nature of which I could not ever so faintly conjecture, but which, I now made no doubt, was that which filled the wood with some nameless terror. Was it material, was it ghostly, or was it (and now some inkling of what Hugh meant began to form itself into my mind) some being that lay on the borderland between the two? Of all the sinister possibilities that appeared the most terrifying.

As we entered the trees again I perceived that reek, alive and yet corrupt, which I had smelt before, but now it was far more potent, and we hurried on, choking with the odour that I now guessed to be not the putrescence of decay, but the living substance of that which crawled and reared itself in the darkness of the wood where no bird would shelter. Somewhere among those trees lurked the reptilian thing that defied and yet compelled credence.

It was a blessed relief to get out of that dim tunnel into the wholesome air of the open and the clear light of evening. Within doors, when we returned, windows were curtained and lamps lit. There was a hint of frost, and Hugh put a match to the fire in his room, where the dogs, still a little apologetic, hailed us with thumpings of drowsy tails.

"And now we've got to talk," said he, "and lay our plans, for whatever it is that is in the wood, we've got to make an end of it. And, if you want to know what I think it is, I'll tell you."

"Go ahead," said I.

"You may laugh at me, if you like," he said, "but I believe it's an elemental. That's what I meant when I said it was a being half-way between the material and the ghostly. I never caught a glimpse of it till this afternoon; I only felt there was something horrible there. But now I've seen it, and it's like what spiritualists and that sort of folk describe as an elemental. A huge phosphorescent slug is what they tell us of it, which at will can surround itself with darkness."

Somehow, now safe within doors, in the cheerful light and warmth of the room, the suggestion appeared merely grotesque. Out there in the darkness of that uncomfortable wood something within me had quaked, and I was prepared to believe any horror, but now commonsense revolted.

"But you don't mean to tell me you believe in such rubbish?" I said. "You might as well say it was a unicorn. What is an elemental, anyway? Who has ever seen one except the people who listen to raps in the darkness and say they are made by their aunts?"

"What is it then?" he asked.

"I should think it is chiefly our own nerves," I said. "I frankly acknowledge I got the creeps when I went through the wood first, and I got them much worse when I went through it with you. But it was just nerves; we are frightening ourselves and each other."

"And are the dogs frightening themselves and each other?" he asked. "And the birds?"

That was rather harder to answer; in fact I gave it up.

Hugh continued.

"Well, just for the moment we'll suppose that something else, not ourselves, frightened us and the dogs and the birds," he said, "and that we did see something like a huge phosphorescent slug. I won't call it an elemental, if you object to that; I'll call it It. There's another thing, too, which the existence of It would explain."

"What's that?" I asked.

"Well, it is supposed to be some incarnation of evil, it is a corporeal form of the devil. It is not only spiritual, it is material to this extent that it can be seen bodily in form, and heard, and, as you noticed, smelt, and, God forbid, handled. It has to be kept alive by nourishment. And that explains perhaps why, every day since I have been here, I've found on that knoll we went up some half-dozen dead rabbits."

"Stoats and weasels," said I.

"No, not stoats and weasels. Stoats kill their prey and eat it. These rabbits have not been eaten; they've been drunk."

"What on earth do you mean?" I asked.

"I examined several of them. There was just a small hole in their throats, and they were drained of blood. Just skin and bones, and a sort of grey mash of fibre, like, like the fibre of an orange which has been sucked. Also there was a horrible smell lingering on them. And was the thing you had a glimpse of like a stoat or a weasel?"

There came a rattle at the handle of the door.

"Not a word to Daisy," said Hugh as she entered.

"I heard you come in," she said. "Where did you go?"

"All round the place," said I, "and came back through the wood. It is odd; not a bird did we see, but that is partly accounted for because it was dark."

I saw her eyes search Hugh's, but she found no communication there. I guessed that he was planning some attack on It next day, and he did not wish her to know that anything was afoot.

"The wood's unpopular," he said. "Birds won't go there, dogs won't go there, and Daisy won't go there. I'm bound to say I share the feeling too, but having braved its terrors in the dark I've broken the spell."

"All quiet, was it?" asked she.

"Quiet wasn't the word for it. The smallest pin could have been heard dropping half a mile off."

We talked over our plans that night after she had gone up to bed. Hugh's story about the sucked rabbits was rather horrible, and though there was no certain connection between those empty rinds of animals and what we had seen, there seemed a certain reasonableness about it. But anything, as he pointed out, which could feed like that was clearly not without its material side—ghosts did not have dinner, and if it was material it was vulnerable.

Our plans, therefore, were very simple; we were going to tramp through the wood, as one walks up partridges in a field of turnips, each with a shot-gun and a supply of cartridges. I cannot say that I looked forward to the expedition, for I hated the thought of getting into closer quarters with that mysterious denizen of the woods; but there was a certain excitement about it, sufficient to keep me awake a long time, and when I got to sleep to cause very vivid and awful dreams.

The morning failed to fulfil the promise of the clear sunset; the sky was lowering and cloudy and a fine rain was falling. Daisy had shopping-errands which took her into the little town, and as soon as she had set off we started on our business. The yellow retriever, mad with joy at the sight of guns, came bounding with us across the garden, but on our entering the wood he slunk back home again.

96

The wood was roughly circular in shape, with a diameter perhaps of half a mile. In the centre, as I have said, there was an open clearing about a quarter of a mile across, which was thus surrounded by a belt of thick trees and copse a couple of hundred yards in breadth. Our plan was first to walk together up the path which led through the wood, with all possible stealth, hoping to hear some movement on the part of what we had come to seek. Failing that, we had settled to tramp through the wood at the distance of some fifty yards from each other in a circular track; two or three of these circuits would cover the whole ground pretty thoroughly. Of the nature of our quarry, whether it would try to steal away from us, or possibly attack, we had no idea; it seemed, however, yesterday to have avoided us.

Rain had been falling steadily for an hour when we entered the wood; it hissed a little in the tree-tops overhead; but so thick was the cover that the ground below was still not more than damp. It was a dark morning outside; here you would say that the sun had already set and that night was falling. Very quietly we moved up the grassy path, where our footfalls were noiseless, and once we caught a whiff of that odour of live corruption; but though we stayed and listened not a sound of anything stirred except the sibilant rain over our heads. We went across the clearing and through to the far gate, and still there was no sign.

"We'll be getting into the trees then," said Hugh. "We had better start where we got that whiff of it."

We went back to the place, which was towards the middle of the encompassing trees. The odour still lingered on the windless air.

"Go on about fifty yards," he said, "and then we'll go in. If either of us comes on the track of it we'll shout to each other."

I walked on down the path till I had gone the right distance, signalled to him, and we stepped in among the trees.

I have never known the sensation of such utter loneliness. I knew that Hugh was walking parallel with me, only fifty yards away, and if I hung on my step I could faintly hear his tread among the beech leaves. But I felt as if I was quite sundered in this dim place from all companionship of man; the only live thing that lurked here was that monstrous mysterious creature of evil. So thick were the trees that I could not see more than a dozen yards in any direction; all places outside the wood seemed infinitely remote, and infinitely remote also everything that had occurred to me in normal human life. I had been whisked out of all wholesome experiences into this antique and evil place. The rain had ceased, it whispered no longer in the tree-tops, testifying that there did exist a world and a sky outside, and only a few drops from above pattered on the beech leaves.

Suddenly I heard the report of Hugh's gun, followed by his shouting voice.

"I've missed it," he shouted; "it's coming in your direction."

I heard him running towards me, the beech-leaves rustling, and no doubt his footsteps drowned a stealthier noise that was close to me. All that happened now, until once more I heard the report of Hugh's gun, happened, I suppose, in less than a minute. If it had taken much longer I do not imagine I should be telling it to-day.

I stood there then, having heard Hugh's shout, with my gun cocked, and ready to put to my shoulder, and I listened to his running footsteps. But still I saw nothing to shoot at and heard nothing. Then between two beech trees, quite close to me, I saw what I can only describe as a ball of darkness. It rolled very swiftly towards me over the few yards that separated me from it, and then, too late, I heard the dead beech-leaves rustling below it. Just before it reached me, my brain realised what it was, or what it might be, but before I could raise my gun to shoot at that nothingness, it was upon me. My gun was twitched out of my hand, and I was enveloped in this blackness, which was the very essence of corruption. It knocked me off my feet, and I sprawled flat on my back, and upon me, as I lay there, I felt the weight of this invisible assailant.

I groped wildly with my hands and they clutched something cold and slimy and hairy. They slipped off it, and next moment there was laid across my shoulder and neck something which felt like an india-rubber tube. The end of it fastened on to my neck like a snake, and I felt the skin rise beneath it. Again, with clutching hands, I tried to tear that obscene strength away from me, and as I struggled with it, I heard Hugh's footsteps close to me through this layer of darkness that hid everything.

My mouth was free, and I shouted at him.

"Here, here!" I yelled "Close to you, where it is darkest."

I felt his hands on mine, and that added strength detached from my neck that sucker that pulled at it. The coil that lay heavy on my legs and chest writhed and struggled and relaxed. Whatever it was that our four hands held, slipped out of them, and I saw Hugh standing close to me. A yard or two off, vanishing among the beech trunks, was that blackness which had poured over me. Hugh put up his gun, and with his second barrel fired at it.

The blackness dispersed, and there, wriggling and twisting like a huge worm lay what we had come to find. It was alive still, and I picked up my gun which lay by my side and fired two more barrels into it. The writhings dwindled into mere shudderings and shakings, and then it lay still.

With Hugh's help I got to my feet, and we both reloaded before going nearer. On the ground there lay a monstrous thing, half-slug, half worm. There was no head to it; it ended in a blunt point with an orifice. In colour it was grey covered with sparse black hairs; its length I suppose was some four feet, its thickness at the broadest part was that of a man's thigh, tapering towards each end. It was shattered by shot at its middle. There were stray pellets which had hit it elsewhere, and from the holes they had made there oozed not blood, but some grey viscous matter.

As we stood there some swift process of disintegration and decay began. It lost outline, it melted, it liquified, and in a minute more we were looking at a mass of stained and coagulated beech leaves. Again and quickly that liquor of corruption faded, and there lay at our feet no trace of what had been there. The overpowering odour passed away, and there came from the ground just the sweet savour of wet earth in springtime, and from above the glint of a sunbeam piercing the clouds. Then a sudden pattering among the dead leaves sent my heart into my mouth again, and I cocked my gun. But it was only Hugh's yellow retriever who had joined us.

We looked at each other.

"You're not hurt?" he said.

I held my chin up.

"Not a bit," I said. "The skin's not broken, is it?"

"No; only a round red mark. My God, what was it? What happened?"

"Your turn first," said I. "Begin at the beginning."

"I came upon it quite suddenly," he said. "It was lying coiled like a sleeping dog behind a big beech. Before I could fire, it slithered off in the direction where I knew you were. I got a snap shot at it among the trees, but I must have missed, for I heard it rustling away. I shouted to you and ran after it. There was a circle of absolute darkness on the ground, and your voice came from the middle of it. I couldn't see you at all, but I clutched at the blackness and my hands met yours. They met something else, too."

We got back to the house and had put the guns away before Daisy came home from her shopping. We had also scrubbed and brushed and washed. She came into the smoking-room.

"You lazy folk," she said. "It has cleared up, and why are you still indoors? Let's go out at once."

I got up.

"Hugh has told me you've got a dislike of the wood," I said, "and it's a lovely wood. Come and see; he and I will walk on each side of you and hold your hands. The dogs shall protect you as well."

"But not one of them will go a yard into the wood," said she.

"Oh yes, they will. At least we'll try them. You must promise to come if they do."

Hugh whistled them up, and down we went to the gate. They sat panting for it to be opened, and scuttled into the thickets in pursuit of interesting smells.

"And who says there are no birds in it?" said Daisy. "Look at that robin! Why, there are two of them. Evidently house-hunting."

X

THE CORNER HOUSE

Firham-by-sea had long been known to Jim Purley and myself, though we had been careful not to talk about it, and for years we had been accustomed to skulk quietly away from London, either alone or together, for a day or two of holiday at that delightful and unheard-of little village. It was not, I may safely say, any secretive or dog-in-the-manger instinct of keeping a good thing to ourselves that was the cause of this reticence, but it was because if Firham had become known at all the whole charm of it would have vanished. A popular Firham, in fact, would cease to be Firham, and while we should lose it nobody else would gain it. Its remoteness, its isolation, its emptiness were its most essential qualities; it would have been impossible, so we both of us felt, to have gone to Firham with a party of friends, and the idea of its little inn being peopled with strangers, or its odd little nine-hole golf-course with the small corrugated-iron shed for its club-house becoming full of serious golfers would certainly have been sufficient to make us desire never to play there again. Nor, indeed, were we guilty of any selfishness in keeping the knowledge of that golf-course to ourselves, for the holes were short and dull and the fairway badly kept. It was only because we were at Firham that we so often strolled round it, losing balls in furse bushes and marshy ground, and considering it quite decent putting if we took no more than three putts on a green. It was bad golf in fact, and no one in his senses would think of going to Firham to play bad golf, when good golf was so vastly more accessible. Indeed, the only reason why I have spoken of the golf-links is because in an indirect and distant manner they were connected with the early incidents of the story which strung itself together there, and which, to me at any rate, has destroyed the secure tranquillity of our remote little hermitage.

To get to Firham at all from London, except by a motor drive of some hundred and twenty miles, is a slow progress, and after two changes the leisurely railway eventually lands you no nearer than five miles from your destination. After that a switch-back road terminating in a long decline brings you off the inland Norfolk hills, and into the broad expanse of lowland, once reclaimed from the sea, and now protected from marine invasion by big banks and dykes. From the top of the last hill you get your first sight of the village, its brick-built houses with their tiled roofs smouldering redly in the sunset, like some small, glowing island anchored in that huge expanse of green, and, a mile beyond it, the dim blue of the sea. There are but few trees to be seen on that wide landscape, and those stunted and slanted in their growth by the prevailing wind off the coast, and the great sweep of the country is composed of featureless fields intersected with drainage dykes, and dotted with sparse cattle. A sluggish stream, fringed with reed-beds and loose-strife, where moor-hens chuckle, passes just outside the village, and a few hundred yards below it is spanned by a bridge and a sluice-gate. From there it broadens out into an estuary, full of shining water at high tide, and of grey mud-banks at the ebb, and passes between rows of tussocked sand-dunes out to sea.

The road, descending from the higher inlands, strikes across these reclaimed marshes, and after a mile of solitary travel enters the village of Firham. To right and left stand a few outlying cottages, whitewashed and thatched, each with a strip of gay garden in front and perhaps a fisherman's net spread out to dry on the wall, but before they form anything that could be called a street the road takes a sudden sharp-angled turn, and at once you are in the square which, indeed, forms the entire village. On each side of the broad cobbled space is a line of houses, on one side a post office and police-station with a dozen small shops where may be bought the more rudimentary needs of existence, a baker's, a butcher's, a tobacconist's. Opposite is a row of little residences midway between villa and cottage, while at the far end stands the dumpy grey church with the vicarage, behind green and rather dilapidated palings, beside it. At the near end is the "Fisherman's Arms," the modest hostelry at which we always put up, flanked by two or three more small red-brick houses, of which the farthest, where the road leaves the square again, is the Corner House of which this story treats.

The Corner House was an object of mild curiosity to Jim and me, for while the rest of the houses in the square, shops and residences alike, had a tidy and well-cared-for appearance, with an air of prosperity on a small contented scale, the Corner House presented a marked and curious contrast. The faded paint on the door was blistered and patchy, the step of the threshold always unwhitened and partly overgrown with an encroachment of moss, as if there was little traffic across it. Over the windows inside were stretched dingy casement curtains, and the Virginia creeper which straggled untended up the discoloured front of the house drooped over the dull panes like the hair over a terrier's eyes. Sometimes in one or other of these windows, between the curtains and the glass, there sat a mournful grey cat, but all day long no further sign of life within gave evidence of occupation. Behind the house was a spacious square of garden enclosed by a low brick wall, and from the upper windows of "The Fisherman's Arms" it was possible to look into it. There was a gravel path running round it, entirely overgrown, and a flower-bed underneath the wall was a jungle of rank weeds among which, in summer, two or three neglected rose trees put out a few meagre flowers. A broken water-butt stood at the end of it, and in the middle a rusty iron seat, but never at morning or at noon or at evening did I see any human figure in it; it seemed entirely derelict and unvisited.

At dusk shabby curtains were drawn across the windows that looked into the square, and then between chinks you could see that one room was lit within. The house, it was evident, had once been a very dignified little residence; it was built of red brick and was early Georgian in date, square and comfortable with its enclosed plot behind; one wondered, as I have said, with mild curiosity what blight had fallen on it, what manner of folk moved silent and unseen behind the dingy casement curtains all day and sat in that front room when night had fallen.

It was not only to us but also to the Firhamites generally that the inhabitants of the Corner House were veiled in some sort of mystery. The landlord of our inn, for instance, in answer to casual questions, could tell us very little of their life nowadays, but what he knew of them indicated that something rather grim lurked behind the drawn curtains. It was a married couple who lived there, and he could remember the arrival of Mr. and Mrs. Labson some ten years before.

"She was a big, handsome woman," he said, "and her age might have been thirty. He was a good deal younger; at that time he looked hardly out of his teens, a slim little slip of a fellow, half a head shorter than his wife. I daresay you've seen him on the golf-links, knocking a ball about by himself, for he goes out there every afternoon."

I had more than once noticed a man playing alone, and carrying a couple of clubs. If he was on a green, and saw us coming up, he always went hurriedly on or stood aside at a little distance, with back turned, and waited for us to pass. But neither of us had paid any particular attention to him.

"She doesn't go out with him?" I asked.

"She never leaves the house at all to my knowledge," said the landlord, "though to be sure it wasn't always like that. When first they came here they were always out together, playing golf or boating or fishing, and in the evening there would be the sound of singing or piano-playing from that front room of theirs. They didn't live here entirely, but came down from London, where they had a house, for two or three months in the summer and perhaps a month at Christmas and another month at Easter. There would be friends staying with them much of the time, and merriment and games always going on, and dancing, too, with a gramophone to play their tunes for them till midnight and later. And then, all of a sudden, five years ago now or perhaps a little more, something happened and everything was changed. Yes, that was a queer thing, and sudden, as I say, like a clap of thunder."

"Interesting," said Jim. "What was it that happened?"

"Well, as we saw it, it was like this," said he, "Mr. and Mrs. Labson were down here together in the summer, and one morning as I passed their door I heard her voice inside scolding and swearing at him or at some one. Him it must have been, as we knew later. All that day she went on at him; it was a wonder to think that a woman had so much breath in her body or so much rage in her mind. Next day all their servants, five or six they kept then, butler and lady's maid and valet and housemaid and cook, were all dismissed and off they went. The gardener got his month's wages, too, and was told he'd be wanted no more, and so there were Mr. and Mrs. Labson alone in the house. But half that day, too, she went on shouting and yelling, so it must have been him she was scolding and swearing at. Like a mad woman she was, and never a word from him. Then there would be silence a bit, and she'd break out again, and day after day it was like that, silence and then that screaming voice of hers. As the weeks went on, silence shut down on them; now and

102

then she'd break out again, even as she does to this day, but a month and more will pass now, and you'll never hear a sound from within the house."

"And what had been the cause of it all?" I asked.

"That came out in the papers," said he, "when Mr. Labson was made a bankrupt. He had been speculating on the Stock Exchange, not with his own money alone, but with hers, and had lost nigh every penny. His house in London was sold, and all they had left was this house which belonged to her, and a bit of money he hadn't got at, which brings them in a pound or two a week. They keep no servants, and every morning Mr. Labson goes out early with his basket on his arm and brings provisions for their dinner with the shilling or two she gives him. They say he does the cooking as well, and the housework too, though there's not too much of that, if you can judge from what you see from outside, while she sits with her hands in her lap doing nothing from morning till night. Sitting there and hating him, you may say."

It was a weird, grim sort of story, and from that moment the house, to my mind, took on, as with a deeper dye of forbiddingness, something of its quality. Its desolate and untended aspect was fully earned, the uncleaned windows and discoloured door seemed a fit expression of the spirit that dwelt there: the house was the faithful expression of those who lived in it, of the man whose folly or knavery had brought them to a penury that was near ruin, and of the woman who was never seen, but sat behind the dirty curtained windows hating him, and making him her drudge. He was her slave; those hours when she screamed and raved at him must surely have broken his spirit utterly, or, whatever his fault had been, he must have rebelled against so servile and dismal an existence. Just that hour or two of remission she gave him in the afternoon that he might get air and exercise to keep his health, and continue his life of bondage, and then back again he went to the seclusion and the simmering hostility.

As sometimes happens when a subject has got started, the round of trivial, everyday experiences begins to bristle with allusions and hints that bear on it, so now when this matter of the Corner House had been set going, Jim and I began to be constantly aware of its ticking. It was just that: it was as if a clock had been wound up and started off, and now we were aware in a way we had not been before that it was steadily ticking on, and the hands silently moving towards some unconjecturable hour. Fancifully, and fantastically enough I wondered what the hour would be towards which the silent pointers were creeping. Would there be some sort of jarring whirr that gave warning that the hour was imminent, or should we miss that, and be suddenly startled by some reverberating shock? Such an idea was, of course, purely an invention of the imagination, but somehow it had got hold of me, and I used to pass the Corner House with an uneasy glance at its dingy windows, as if they were the dial that interpreted the progress of the sombre mechanism within.

The reader must understand that all this formed no continuous series of impressions. Jim and I were at Firham only on short visits, with intervals of weeks or even of months in between. But certainly after the subject had been started we had more frequent glimpses of Mr. Labson. Day after day we saw his flitting figure on the links, keeping its distance, and retreating before us, but once we approached close up to him before he was aware of our presence. It was an afternoon that threatened rain, and in order to be nearer shelter if the storm burst suddenly we had cut two holes and walked across an intervening tract of rough ground to a hole which took us in a homeward direction. He was just addressing his ball on this teeing-ground when, looking up, he saw that we were beside him; he gave a little squeal as of terror, picked up his ball, and scuttled away, at a shuffling run, with abject terror written on his lean white face. Not a word did he give us in answer to Jim's begging him to precede us, not once did he look round.

"But the man's quaking with fear," said I, as he disappeared. "He could hardly pick up his ball."

"Poor devil!" said Jim. "There's something formidable at the Corner House."

He had hardly spoken when the rain began in torrents, and we trotted with the best speed of middle-aged gentlemen towards the corrugated-iron shed of the club-house. But Mr. Labson did not join us there for shelter; for we saw him plodding homewards through the downpour rather than face his fellow-creatures.

That close glimpse of Mr. Labson had made the affair of the Corner House much more real. Behind the curtains where the light was lit in the evening there sat a man in whose soul terror was enthroned. Was it terror of his companion who sat there with him that reigned so supreme that even when he was away out on the links it still was master of him? Had it also so drained from him all dregs of manhood and of courage that he could not even run away, but must return to the grim house for fear of his fear, as a rabbit on whose track is a weasel has not the courage to gallop off and easily save itself from the sharp white teeth? Or were there ties of affection between him and the woman whom his folly had brought to penury, so that as a willing penance he cooked and drudged for her? And then I thought of the voice that had yelled at him all day; it was more likely that, as Jim had said, there was something formidable at the Corner House, before which he cowered and from which he had not the strength to fly.

There were other glimpses of him as, with his basket on his arm in the early morning, he brought home bread and milk and some cheap cut from the butcher's. Once I saw him enter his house on his return from his marketing. He must have locked the door before going out, for now he unlocked it again, slipped in, and I heard the key click in the wards again. Once, too, though only in featureless outline, I saw her who shared his solitude, for passing by the Corner House in the dusk, the lamp had been lit within, and I had a glimpse through the thin casement blinds of a carpetless room, a blackened ceiling and one big armchair drawn up to the fire. And at that moment the form of a woman silhouetted itself between me and the light. She was very tall, and immensely broad and stout, and her hands, large as a man's, grasped the curtain. Next moment, with a jingle of running rings, she had drawn it, and shut up herself and the man for the long winter evening and the night that followed.

The same evening, I remember, Jim had occasion to go to the post office and came back to our snug little sitting-room with something of horror in his eyes.

"You've seen her to-day," he said, "and I've heard her."

"Who? Oh! at the Corner House?" I asked.

"Yes. I was just passing it, when she began. I tell you it scared me. It was scarcely like a human voice at all, or at any rate not like a sane voice. A shrill, swearing gabble all on one note, and going on without a pause. Maniac."

The conjectured picture of the two grew more grim. It was an awful thought that behind those dingy curtains in the bare room there were the pair of them, the little terrified man, and that greater monster of a woman, yelling and bawling at him. Yet what could we do? It seemed impossible to interfere in any way. It was not the business of a couple of visitors from London to intrude on the domestic differences of total strangers. And yet the sequel showed that any interference would have been justified.

The day following was wet from morning till night. A gale of rain mingled with sleet roared in from the north-east, and neither of us stirred abroad, but kept close by the fire listening to the wind bugling in the chimney, and the gale flinging the sheets of water solidly against the window-pane. But after nightfall the wind abated and the sky cleared, and when I went up to bed, sleepy with the day indoors, I saw the shadows of the window bars black against a brightness outside, and pulling up the blind looked on to a blaze of moonlight. Below, a little to the left, was the neglected garden of the Corner House, and there, standing on the grass-grown path, was the figure of the woman I had seen in black silhouette against the lamplight in her room. Now the moonlight shone full on her face and my breath caught in my throat as I looked on that appalling countenance. It was fat and bloated beyond belief, the eyes were but slits above her cheeks, and the lines of her mouth were invisible in their shadows. But even the whiteness of the moonlight gave no pallor to her face, for it was flushed with some purplish hue that seemed nearly black. One glimpse only I had for perhaps she had heard the rattle of my blind, and she looked up and next minute had stepped back into the house again. But that moment was enough; I felt that I had looked on something hellish, something almost outside the wide range of humanity. It was not only the appalling physical ugliness of that monstrous face that was so shocking; it was the expression in the eyes and mouth, visible in that second when she raised her face to look upwards to my window. An inhuman hatred and cruelty were there that made the heart quake; the featureless outline was filled in with details more awful than I had ever conjectured.

We were out on the links again next afternoon on a day of liquid sunshine and brisk air, but some nameless oppression of the spirits held me sundered from the genial and bracing warmth. The idea of that frightened little man being imprisoned all day and night, but for his brief outing, with her who at any moment might break into that screaming torrent of speech, was like a nightmare that came between me and the sun. It would have been something to have seen him out to-day, and know that he was having a respite from that terrible presence; but we caught no sight of him, and when we returned and passed the Corner House the curtains were already drawn, and, as usual, there was silence within.

Jim touched me on the arm as we walked by the windows.

"But there's no light inside this evening," he said.

This was quite true; the curtains were torn, as I knew, in half a dozen places, but neither through these holes nor from the chinks at their edges was there any light showing. Somehow this gave an added horror, which set my nerves jangling.

"Well, we can't knock and tell them they've forgotten to light the lamp," I said.

We had halted for a moment, and even as I spoke I saw coming across the square towards us in the gathering dusk the figure of the man whom we had missed on the links that afternoon. Though I had not seen him approach, nor heard the noise of his footfall on the cobbles, he was now within a few yards of us.

"Here _he_ is anyhow," I said.

Jim turned.

"Where?" he asked.

We were standing perhaps two yards apart, and as he asked that the man stepped between us and advanced to the door of the Corner House. And then, instantaneously, I saw that Jim and I were alone. The door of the Corner House had not opened, but there was no one there.

Jim gave a startled exclamation.

"What was that?" he said. "Something brushed by me."

"Didn't you see anything?" I asked.

"No, but I felt something. I don't know what it was."

"I saw him," said I.

My jangled nerves seemed to have infected Jim.

"Nonsense!" he said. "How could you have seen him? Where has he gone if you saw him? And I don't know what we're standing here for."

Before I could answer I heard from within the Corner House the sound of heavy and shuffling steps; a key grated in the lock, and the door was flung open. Out of it, panting and heaving with some strange agitation, came the woman I had seen last night in her garden.

She had shut the door and locked it before she saw us. She was hatless and shod in great carpet slippers the heels of which tapped on the pavement as she moved, and on her face was the vacancy of some nameless terror. Her mouth, a cavern in that mountain of flesh, was wide, and now there came from it something between a gasp and a rattle. Then, seeing us, quick as a lizard, she whisked round again, fumbled for a moment with the key which she still held in her hand, and there once more was the shut door and the empty pavement. The whole scene passed like a blink of strong light seen in the dusk and vanishing again. She had come out, driven by some terror of her own; she had gone back in terror, it would seem, of us.

It was without a word passing between us that we went back to the inn. Just then there was nothing to be said; for myself, at least. I knew that there was, covering my brain, so to speak, some frozen surface of abject fear which must be thawed. I knew that I had seen, I knew that Jim had felt, something which had no tangible existence in the material world. He had felt what I had seen, and I had seen the form and bodily semblance of the man who lived at the Corner House. But what his wife had seen that drove her from the house, and why, seeing us, she had whisked back into it again I had no notion. Perhaps when a certain physical horror in my brain was uncongealed I should know.

Presently we were sitting in the small, cosy room, with our tea ready for us, and the fire burning bright on the hearth. We talked, odd as it may appear, of anything else but _that_. But the silences between the abandonment of our topic and the introduction of another grew longer, and at last Jim spoke.

"Something has happened," he said. "You saw what wasn't there, and I felt what wasn't there. What did we see or feel? And what did _she_ see or feel?"

He had hardly spoken when there came a rap at the door, and our landlord entered. For the moment, during which the door was open, I heard from the bar of the inn a shrill, gabbling voice, which I had never heard before, but which I knew Jim had heard.

"There's Mrs. Labson come into the bar, gentlemen," he said, "and she wants to know if it was you who were standing outside her house ten minutes ago. She's got a notion——"

He paused.

"It's hard to make out what she's after," he said. "Her husband has not been at home all day, and he's not home yet, and she thinks you may have seen him on the golf-links. And then she says she's thinking of letting her house for a month, and wonders if you would care to take it, but she runs on so——"

The door opened again, and there she stood, filling the doorway. She had on her head a great feathered hat, and over her shoulders a red satin evening cloak, now moth-eaten and ragged, while on her feet were still those carpet slippers.

"So odd it must seem to you for a lady to intrude like this," she said, "but you are the gentlemen, are you not, whom I saw admiring my house just now?"

Her eyes, now utterly vacant, now suddenly keen and searching, fell on the window. The curtains were not drawn and outside the last of the daylight was fading. She shuffled quickly across the floor and rattled the blind down, first peering out into the dusk.

"I'm sure I don't wonder at that," she gabbled on, "for my house is much admired by visitors here. I was thinking of letting it for a few weeks, though I am not sure that it would be convenient to do so just yet, and even if I did, I should have to put some of my treasures away in a little attic at the top of the house, and lock that up. Some heirlooms, you understand. But that's all by the way. I came in, a very odd intrusion I know, to ask if either of you had seen my husband, Mr. Labson—I am Mrs. Labson, as I should have told you—if you'd seen him on the golf-links this afternoon. He went out about two o'clock, and he's not been back. Most unusual, for there's his tea ready for him always at half-past four."

She paused and seemed to listen intently, then went across to the window again and drew the blind aside.

"I thought I heard a step in my garden just out there," she said, "and I wondered if it was Mr. Labson. Such a pleasant little garden, a bit over-grown maybe; I think I saw one of you gentlemen looking down into it last night, when I was taking a breath of air. Or even if you didn't care to take the whole of my house, perhaps you would like a couple of rooms there. I could make everything most comfortable for you, for Mr. Labson always said I was a wonderful cook and manager, and not a word of complaint have I ever had from him all these years. Still, if he's taken it into his head to go off suddenly like this, I should be pleased to have a lodger in the house, for I'm not accustomed to be alone. Being alone in a house was a thing I never could bear."

She turned to our landlord:

"I'll take a room here for to-night," she said, "if Mr. Labson doesn't come back. Perhaps you would send across for a bag into which I have put what I shall want. No; that would never do; I'll go and get it myself, if you would be so good as to come with me as far as the door. One never knows who is about at this time of night. And if Mr. Labson should come here to look for me, don't let him in whatever you do. Say I'm not here; say I've left home for a day or two and have given no address. You don't want Mr. Labson here, for he's not got a penny of his own, and couldn't pay for his board and lodging, and I won't support him in idleness any longer. He ruined me and I'll be even with him yet. I told him——"

The stream of insane babble suddenly ceased; her eyes, fixing themselves on a dusky corner of the room behind where I stood, grew wide with terror, and her mouth gaped. Simultaneously I heard a gasp of startled amazement from Jim, and turned quickly to see what he and Mrs. Labson were looking at.

There he stood, he whom I had seen half an hour ago appearing suddenly in the square, and as suddenly disappearing as he came to the Corner House. Next minute she had flung the door wide and bolted out. Jim and I followed and saw her rush down the passage outside, and through the open door of the bar into the square. Terror winged her feet, and that great misshapen bulk sped away and was lost in the darkness of the fallen night.

We went straight to the police office, and the country was scoured for the mad woman who, I felt sure, was also a murderess. The river was dragged, and about midnight two fishermen found the body below the sluice-gate at the head of the estuary. Search meantime had been made in the Corner House, and her husband's corpse was discovered, strangled with a silk handkerchief, behind the water-butt in the corner of the garden. Close by was a half-dug excavation, where no doubt she had intended to bury him.

XI

CORSTOPHINE

Fred Bennett had proposed himself for a visit of a couple of nights, and had said in his letter that he had a curious story to tell me. The date he suggested was perfectly convenient, and he arrived just before dinner. We were alone, but when I hinted that I was more than ready to hear his curious story he said that would come later.

"I want to clear the ground first," he said, "for it is always better to agree or disagree on a principle before you advance your illustration."

"Spook?" I asked, knowing that the occult side of life is far more real to him than the happenings of normal existence.

"I really don't know whether you'll think it is spooky or not," he said. "You may think it is only a coincidence. But, you see, I don't believe in coincidences. There isn't such a thing as blind chance, to my mind: what we call chance is only the working out of a law which we are ignorant of."

"Explain," said I.

"Well, take the rising of the sun. If we were ignorant of the movement of the earth, we should think it a coincidence that the sun will rise to-morrow very nearly at the same time as it rose to-day. But we don't call it a coincidence because we know, more or less, the law that makes it do so. That's clear, isn't it?"

"That will do for the present," I said. "I won't argue yet."

"Right. Now since we know about the movement of the earth, we can safely prophesy that the sun will rise to-morrow. Our knowledge of what is past makes us able to see into the future, and, in fact, we shouldn't call it prophecy at all if we were told the sun would rise to-morrow. In just the same way, if a man had known the exact movement of a certain iceberg, and the exact course of the 'Titanic,' he would have been able to prophesy that the 'Titanic' would founder on that iceberg at a certain moment. Our knowledge of the future, in a word, depends entirely on our knowledge of the past, and if we knew absolutely all about the past, we should know absolutely all about the future."

"Not quite," said I. "A fresh factor might come in."

"But that factor would be dependent on the past, too," he said.

"Is the story going to be as difficult as the preliminaries?" I asked.

He laughed.

"Much more difficult," he said. "At least the explanation is much more difficult, if you don't accept these very simple facts. To my mind the idea that the past and present and future are all really one is the only possible way of accounting for it."

He pushed back his plate, and leaned his elbows on the table, looking fixedly at me. He has the most extraordinary eyes I have ever seen: they seem sometimes to look quite through what they are regarding, and then to come back as from some remote focus to your face again.

"Of course time, the whole sum of time, cannot be more than an infinitesimal point in eternity," he said, "even if it is as much as that. When we get out of time, when we die, in fact, we shall regard time as just a point, visible all round, so to speak. Some people, even now, get glimpses of it in its entirety. We call them clairvoyants: they have visions of the future which are actually and literally fulfilled. Or, perhaps, they have, when they see such things, some revelation of the past which enables them, like the man prophesying about the sinking of the 'Titanic,' to foretell the future. If he had found people to believe him a disaster like that might have been averted. Take it which way you like."

Now Fred, as I already knew, had more than once in his life experienced this mysterious enlightenment, and I guessed now the nature of the curious story of which he had spoken.

"You've seen something," I said, rising. "I long to hear all about it."

The night was very hot, and instead of adjourning to another room, we went out into the garden, where there was some coolness of breeze and dew. The sun was set, but light still lingered in the sky, screeching companies of swifts wheeled overhead, and the warmth drew out in subtle distillation the fragrance from the rose-beds. My servant had already put out a little encampment of basket-chairs and a table with cards, if we felt so disposed, on the lawn, and here we settled ourselves.

"And above all things," I said, "tell me your story fully and at length. Otherwise I shall only be asking questions as to details, and that will interrupt you."

With his permission I give the story very much as he told it me. As he spoke the night darkened round us, the swifts ceased their shrill foraging, and bats took their place with shriller and barely audible squeakings. Occasionally there was the flare of a lit match, and the creak of a basket-chair, but there was no other interruption.

"One evening about three weeks ago," he said, "I was dining with Arthur Temple. His wife and his sister-in-law were there, but about half-past ten they went out to a ball. He hates dancing as much as I do, and proposed that we should have a game of chess. I adore chess, and play it quite atrociously, but when I am playing chess I can think of nothing whatever else. That night, however, things went strangely well, and with trembling excitement I saw that after some twenty moves the unwonted prospect of winning my game was opening out in front of me. I mention this to show that I was very wide-awake and concentrated on what I was doing.

"As I meditated the move which was soon to prove fatal to my adversary, a vision such as I have had once or twice before leaped into being before my eyes. My hand was raised to take hold of my queen, when the chess-board at which I was looking and my actual surroundings entirely vanished, and I was standing on the platform of a railway station. There was a train drawn up by it, out of which I was aware I had just stepped, and I knew I had an hour to wait for the one that was to take me on to my unknown destination. Just opposite me was the board on which was painted the name of the station; this I shall not tell you at present, because you might guess what my story is going to be. But though it seemed perfectly natural that I should be there, I had never at that time, to the best of my knowledge, heard of the name of the station before. There was my luggage on the platform, and I gave it in charge of a porter who was exactly like Arthur Temple, told him that I was going for a walk, and would be back before my train was due.

"It was a very dark afternoon—somehow I knew it was afternoon—and the air oppressively close and sultry, as if a storm was coming up. I walked through the booking office of the station and out into a big yard. To the right were some allotment gardens, beyond which the ground rose rapidly up to a distant line of moors, to the left were rows upon rows of sheds, with tall chimneys vomiting smoke, and in front a long street with huddled houses stretching right and left. They were built of grey discoloured stone, with slate roofs, mean and dismal dwellings, and neither in the station-yard nor in the long perspective of the street in front of me was there a sign of any human being. Probably, I thought, the men and women of the place were

111

engaged in those manufacturing buildings, but there were no children playing on the pavements. The place seemed absolutely deserted, and somehow disquieting and appalling.

"I stood there a moment, hesitating as to whether I should start on a walk among such charmless surroundings or stop in the station and while away the hour with my book. Then I became aware that there was waiting for me something which very closely concerned me, and that whatever it was it lay beyond that long untenanted street. I had to go, though I had no idea where I was going or what I should find. I crossed the yard and started to walk up the street.

"As soon as I got on the move that sense of being obliged to go completely vanished; it had given me the required push, I suppose, and I realised that I was just waiting for my train and filling in the time. The street stretched endlessly in front of me, up a steepish hill, and on each side were these low, two-storied houses. Their doors and windows, in spite of the stifling heat, were all shut, and never a face showed from within, nor was there a single footstep but my own to break the silence. No sparrow fluttered in the eaves or foraged in the gutters; no cat slunk along the house-walls or blinked on the doorsteps; there was nothing visible nor audible of the evidence of life.

"On and on I walked, and presently the street began to show signs of coming to an end. The houses on one side ceased, and I looked over long stretches of grimy fields, tenantless of any grazing beasts. At that, like a blink of distant lightning, there flashed on my mind the notion that I did not see any living things because I no longer had anything to do with the living. All about me probably were children and men and women, and cats and sparrows, but I did not belong to them. I was there in some other capacity, and whatever it was that was of significance for me in this desolate place it was not concerned with life. I can't express it more definitely than that, because the notion itself was indefinite, and it flashed upon me but for a moment and was gone again. Then the houses on the other side of the street came to an end also, and I was walking along a black country road, with stunted hedges on each side. Meantime the dusk was coming rapidly on, a thick and murky dusk, hot and windless. The road made a sharp right-angled turn, and while it was open to the fields on one side the other was bounded by a high stone wall that rose above my head. I was beginning to wonder what this enclosure was when I came to a big iron gate in it, and I saw through the bars that it was a graveyard. Row upon row the tombstones glimmered faintly in the dusk, and at the far end of it only just visible in the gathering darkness were the roofs and small spire of a cemetery chapel. The gate was open, and feeling that there was something here which concerned me, I entered and began walking up an unweeded gravel path in the direction of the chapel. As I did this, I looked at my watch and saw that half of my hour of waiting was nearly spent, and that I must soon be retracing my steps. But I knew I had business here which must be performed.

112

"The tombstones came to an end, and there was a broad space of open grass between me and the chapel. Then I saw that there was one grave standing alone there, and with that odd curiosity that prompts us to read the names on tombstones I left the path and went to it.

"Though it appeared rather new, glimmering whitely in the dusk, I saw that already moss and lichen had covered the face of it, and I wondered whether it was the grave of some stranger who had died a lonely death here, and had no one, friend or relation, who looked after it. The name, whatever it was, was quite overgrown, and with some impulse of pity for him who lay below, and had so soon been forgotten, I began scraping it with the ferule of my stick. The moss peeled off quite easily, coming away in long shreds and fibres, and presently I saw that the name was visible. But as I worked the darkness had so gathered that I could not read it, and I lit a match and held it to the surface of the stone. And the name I read there was my own.

"I heard myself give some exclamation of surprise and horror, and immediately afterwards I heard Arthur Temple's laugh, and then again I was in his room, staring at the chess-board, and looking with dismay at the move he had made. I had not anticipated that, and my wonderful plan was ruined.

"'For half a minute,' he said, 'I thought you had got me.' A few moves were sufficient to bring the game to a most undesired conclusion, and after a short chat I went home. The vision apparently had lasted just the space of his own move, for mine was already being made when it began."

He paused, and I supposed the story was over.

"What an odd affair," I said, "it's just one of those meaningless but interesting intrusions into everyday life, coming from God knows where, which doesn't lead to anything. What was the name of the station, by the way? Did you take the trouble to find out whether your vision resembled the actual place? Was that the coincidence?"

I was, I confess, rather disappointed, though indeed, he had been telling his story very well. But like so many of these strange glimpses which clairvoyants and mediums seem genuinely to get into the world of powers and unseen agencies, which we know lies so closely round us, and sometimes manifests itself to the senses of those who are still on the material plane, it seemed so pointless. Even if it turned out that eventually he was buried in the cemetery of this twilit, untenanted town, what good would it have done him to have known of that before it happened? What is the use of communications between this world and some other world inaccessible to the ordinary perceptions of mankind if these communications contain nothing that is of value or interest?

He looked at me with that distant penetrating glance, which seemed to be focused on some inconceivable remoteness, and laughed.

"No, that wasn't the coincidence," he said, "at least that coincidence, if you call it so, is not the point of the story. As for the name of the station, that will come very soon now."

"Oh, there is more then, is there?" I asked.

"Certainly, you told me to tell it you at length. That's only the prologue, or the first act. Shall I go on?"

"Yes, of course. Sorry."

"Well there I was again in Arthur's room, the whole vision had lasted perhaps a minute, and he was quite unaware that I had done anything but stare at the chess-board, and when he made that move which upset my plans, give a cry of surprise and dismay.... And then as I told you, we talked for a little, and he mentioned that he and his wife were possibly going up to Yorkshire for Whitsuntide, to a place called Helyat, which she had lately inherited on the death of an uncle. It was up on the moors, he said, with a little shooting in the autumn, and just now some rather good trout fishing. If they went, they would be there for a fortnight or so; perhaps I would come up for a week, if I was doing nothing particular. I said I should be delighted to, but this was contingent, of course, on their going, and the matter was left vague. I saw neither of them again, nor did I hear any more till, ten days afterwards, I got a telegram from him—he always sends a telegram in preference to a letter, because he says it receives more attention—asking me to come up as soon as ever I liked. If I would let him know the day and the time of my train, they would meet me: their station was Helyat. Helyat, I may say, was not the name of the station in the vision I have told you."

"There was an ABC time-table in the house, I looked out Helyat, found a train that started and arrived at convenient hours, and I telegraphed to Arthur that I would travel by it next day. So that was settled.

"The weather in London that week had been extremely oppressive, and I welcomed the idea of getting up on to the Yorkshire moors. Moreover, since the day when I had experienced that odd vision I had gone about with a strong sense of some impending disaster. I told myself in the way one does, that the heat and sultriness of town were responsible for my depressed spirits, but I knew very well that it was the vision that lay at the root of them. I never shook off the consciousness of it, it lay like some leaden weight upon me, it got between the normal sunlight of life and myself like some menacing thunder-cloud. And now, the moment that I had sent off that telegram, the exhilaration at the thought of getting into a high and bracing air completely passed, and the dread of some imminent peril took such

114

possession of me that I very nearly sent a second telegram on the heels of the first to say that I could not manage to come after all. But why I connected these forebodings with my journey or my stay at Helyat I had no idea, and search my mind as I might there was no conceivable reason for doing so. I told myself that this was one of those causeless fears which sometimes obsess people of the steadiest nerves, and that to yield to it was to take a definite step in the direction of mental unbalance. It would never do to let oneself become the prey of such unreasonable terrors.

"I made up my mind therefore to go through it with, not only for the sake of not losing a pleasant week in the country, but even more for the sake of proving to myself the unreasonableness of my fears. I arrived accordingly at the terminus next morning, with a quarter of an hour to spare, found a corner seat, engaged a place in the restaurant-car for lunch, and settled down. Just before the train started the ticket-inspector came round, and as he clipped my ticket, looked at the name of my destination.

"'Change at Corstophine, sir,' he said, and now you know the name of the station at which I alighted in that vision.

"I felt panic invading my very bones, but I asked one question.

"'Do I wait there long?' I said.

"He consulted a time-table which he pulled out of his pocket.

"'Just an hour, sir,' he said. 'A branch line takes you on to Helyat.'"

I broke my determination not to interrupt him.

"Corstophine?" I said, "I've seen that name lately in the paper."

"So have I. We're just coming to that," said he. "And then the panic grew beyond my control. I could not resist it any longer, and I got out of the train. With some difficulty I managed to obtain my luggage from the van, and I sent a telegram to Arthur Temple saying I was detained. A minute later the train started, and there I was on the platform, already terribly ashamed of myself, but knowing in some interior cell of my brain that I was right in doing what I had done. In some manner, as yet inscrutable to me, I had obeyed the warning which I had received ten days ago.

"I dined that evening at my club, and after dinner read in an evening paper about a terrible railway accident that had occurred during the afternoon at Corstophine. The fast train from London, by which I should have travelled, stopped there at 2.53 p.m.; the train taking the branch line which goes up into the moors and stops at Helyat was due to start at 3.54; it starts, so said the account, from the down platform, crosses on to the up line along which it runs for some hundred yards, and then branches off to the right. About the same time an up-express is due to pass through Corstophine without stopping. Usually the local train to Helyat waits on the down-line for it to pass; this afternoon, however, the express was late, and the Helyat train was signalled to start. Whether owing to a mistake of the signalman, who had not put up the signal against the express, or whether the driver of the express had not seen it, was not yet clear, but what had happened was that while the Helyat train was on the section of the up-line, the express, running at full speed to make up time, dashed into it. The engine and front carriage of the express was wrecked, and the other train reduced simply to matchwood: the express had gone through it like a bullet."

Again he paused; this time I did not interrupt.

"So, there was my vision," he said, "and there was the interpretation of the warning it sent me. But there remains a little more to tell you, which, to my mind, is as curious from the point of view of the scientific investigator of such phenomena as anything yet. It is this:

"I instantly made up my mind to start for Helyat next day. Vision and fulfilment alike, as far as I was concerned, had done their work, and I had an immense curiosity to ascertain whether all the imagery and scenery of the vision had an actual existence here on earth, or whether it was an impulse, so to speak, from the immaterial world, clothing itself in forms of time and space. I must confess that I hoped it was the former, that I should find at Corstophine what I imagined I had seen there, for that would show me how closely the two worlds are interlinked or dovetailed together, so that the one can use for our mortal sense the scenery of the other.... So I telegraphed again to Arthur Temple, saying that I should arrive at the same hour next day.

"Again, therefore, I went to the London terminus, and again the ticket inspector told me I must change at Corstophine. The papers that morning were full of this terrible accident, but he assured me that the line was already clear, and that I should get through. An hour before we were due there we passed into the black country of collieries and manufacture, the sun was hidden in the murk of the smoke-belching chimneys, and when we stopped at the station where I was to change, the earth was shrouded under that gross and unnatural twilight in which I had seen it before. And exactly as before, I gave my luggage in charge of the porter, and set out to explore a place I had never seen but knew with a vividness which no normal exercise of memory can give. There, on the right of the station yard, were the allotment gardens, behind which rose the line of moors, among which, no doubt, Helyat lay, and there, to the left, were the roofs of sheds, with tall chimneys vomiting smoke, and there in front of me was the mean steep street stretching into an endless perspective. But to-day, instead of finding a dead and uninhabited town, it was full of busy crowds hurrying about. Children were playing in the gutters; cats sat and made their toilets on doorsteps; the sparrows pecked at the refuse heaps that strewed the road. That seemed natural; when my spirit, or my astral body or whatever you care to call it, visited Corstophine before I belonged, potentially, to the dead, and the living were outside my ken. Now, potentially, I belonged to the living, and they swarmed about me.

"I went quickly up the street, for from my previous experience I knew that there was not more than time to go to the place which I must visit, and return to catch my train. It was swelteringly hot, and curiously dark: the darkness increased every moment as I hurried along. Then the houses on the left came to an end, and I looked over grimy fields, and then the houses on the right ceased also, and the road made a sharp turn. Presently I was walking below the stone wall, too high to look over, and there was the iron gate ajar, and the rows of tombstones within, and against the blackened sky the roofs and spire of the cemetery chapel. Once more I passed up the grass-grown gravel, and there was an empty space in front of the chapel, with just one gravestone standing apart from the rest.

"I crossed the grass to it and saw that it was overgrown with moss and lichen. I scraped with my stick the surface of the stone on which was cut the name of the man who lay below it—or woman, maybe—and then, lighting a match, for it was impossible to read the letters in the darkness, I saw that it was my own name and none other that was chiselled there. There was no date, there was no text; there was just my name and nothing else."

He paused again. Sometime during the course of his story, my servant must have brought out a tray of syphons and whisky, and put on the table a lamp that now burned there unwaveringly in the still air. But I had not been aware of his coming or going; I had known no more of it than Fred had known of his opponent's move at chess while the vision filled the field of his conscious perceptions. He helped himself to something, I did the same, and he spoke again.

"It is arguable," he said, "that at some time in my life I had been to Corstophine, and had done exactly what I did in my vision. I can't prove that I haven't, because I can't account for every day that I have spent since I was born. I can only say that I have absolutely no recollection of having done so, or of ever having heard of such a place as Corstophine. But if I had, it is on the cards that my vision was only a recollection, and that its preventing my going to Corstophine on a particular day when, if I had gone there, I should certainly have been killed in a railway accident was only a coincidence. If that had happened, and if my body had been identified, my remains would certainly have been buried in that cemetery, because my executor would have found in my will the wish that, unless there were strong reasons for the contrary, I should be buried in the graveyard nearest to the place in which I had died. Naturally I don't care what happens to my body when I have done with it, and I don't want it to be a sentimental nuisance to other people."

He sat up, stretched himself, and laughed.

"That would have been a very elaborate coincidence," he said, "and the coincidence would have had a longer arm than ever, if they had observed that close to my grave there was buried another Fred Bennett. I must say that the simpler explanation appeals to me more."

"And what is the simpler explanation?" I asked.

"The one that you really believe in, though your reason revolts against it because it has not the faintest idea of the law that lies behind it. It's a law all the same, though it doesn't manifest itself so often as that which governs the rising of the sun. Let's say, then, that it's a law loosely analogous to that which regulates the appearance of comets, though of course it is far more frequent in its manifestations. Perhaps it requires for its manifestation a certain psychical perception given to some people and not to others, just in the same way as it requires a certain physical perception to hear the squeal of those bats which are flitting overhead. I can't hear them personally, but I think you told me before that you can. I perfectly accept your word for it, though the noise doesn't reach my senses."

"And the law?" I asked.

"The law is that in the real world, in the true existence beyond the 'muddy vesture of decay,' the past and the present and the future are one. They are a point in eternity which can be perceived and handled all round. Difficult to express, but that's the kind of thing. Occasionally, and in the case of some people the muddy vesture can be stripped off, though only intermittently and for a moment, and then they perceive and know. It's very simple really, and, as a matter of fact, you believe it all the time."

"I know I do," said I, "but just because it is so rare, and because it is so abnormal, I want to try to account for everything of the sort which I hear by an extension of the physical senses. Thought reading, telepathy, suggestion: all these are natural phenomena. We know a little about them, and we've got to exclude them first before we accept anything so strange as a vision of the future."

"Exclude them, then," he said. "I'm quite with you. But you mustn't think that I put clairvoyance or knowledge of the future on a different plane to any of those. It's only an extension of a natural law, a branch line, so to speak, that led to Helyat, off the main line. It's part of the system."

There was something to think about there, and we were both silent. I could hear the squeak of the bats, and Fred couldn't, but I should have thought it very materialistic of him to deny that I heard them just because his ears were deaf to them. I thought over the story, point by point; and, as he had said, I knew I really agreed with him on the principle that from somewhere out of what we think of as the great void, merely because we do not rightly know what is there, there did come, and had come, and would come these wireless messages to the receivers that were in tune with them. There was the dead town of his vision, uninhabited, because potentially he was of the dead, and then it became a live town, because, having taken the warning, he was of the living. And then a bright and brilliant and go-to-bed notion struck me.

"Ha! I've picked a hole," I said. "When you saw the vision, Corstophine was without inhabitants, because you were dead. Wasn't it so?"

He laughed again.

"I know exactly what you are going to ask," he said. "You're going to ask about the porter at the station to whom I gave my luggage. I can't explain that. Perhaps his appearance was like the last conscious view of the anæsthetist, who stands by you when you are having gas, and is the final link with the material world. He was like Arthur Temple, you will remember."

XII

THE TEMPLE

Frank Ingleton and I had left London early in July with the intention of spending a couple of months at least in Cornwall. This sojourn was not by any means to be a complete holiday, for he was a student of those remains of prehistoric civilisation which are found in such mysterious abundance in the ancient county, and I was employed on a book which should have already been approaching completion, but which was still lamentably far from its consummation. Naturally there was to be a little golf and a little sea-bathing for relaxation, but we were both keen on our work and meant to have gathered in a respectable harvest of industry before we returned.

The village of St. Caradoc, from all accounts, seemed likely to be favourable to our projects, for there were remains in the neighbourhood which had never been thoroughly investigated by any archæologist, and its position on the map, remote from any of the more celebrated holiday centres, promised a reasonable tranquillity. It supplied also the desirable relaxations; the club-house of a pleasantly hazardous golf-course stood at the bottom of the hotel garden, and five minutes' walk across the sand-dunes among which the holes were placed, led to the beach. The hotel was comfortable, and at present half-empty, and fortune seemed to smile on our undertakings. We settled down, therefore, without further plans. Frank meant, before he left, to visit other parts of the county, but here, within a mile of the hotel, was that curious circle of monoliths, like some Stonehenge in miniature, known as the "Council of Penruth." It had always been supposed, so Frank told me, that it was some place of Druidical worship, but he distrusted the conclusion and wanted to study it minutely on the spot.

I went there with him by way of an evening saunter on the second day after our arrival. The shortest way was along the sand-dunes, and thence up a steep, grassy slope on to the ploughed stretches of the uplands. In that warm, soft climate the wheat was in full ear, and beginning already to turn ripe and tawny. A very narrow path led across these cornfields to our destination, and from far off one could see the circle of stones, four to five feet high, standing there, black and austere, against the yellowing grain. Though all the country round was in cultivation no plough had furrowed the interior of the circle, and inside was the ancient turf of the downs, short and velvety, with patches of thyme and hare-bells. It seemed odd; a plough could have passed backwards and forwards between the monoliths and a half-acre of land have been made fruitful.

"But why isn't it ploughed?" I asked.

"Oh, you're in the land of superstitions and ancient sorceries," he said. "These circles are never touched or made use of. And do you see, the path across the fields by which we have come passes round it; it doesn't run across it. There it goes again on the far side, pursuing the same line, after making the detour."

He laughed.

"The farmer of the land was up here this morning when I was making some measurements," he said. "He went round it, I noticed, and when his dog came inside after some interesting smell, he called it back, and cuffed it, and rapped out: 'Come out of that there; and never do you go within again.'"

"But what's the idea?" I asked.

"Something clings to it, some curse, some abomination. They think no doubt, just as the archæologists do, that the place has been a Druidical temple, where dreadful rites were performed and human sacrifices made. But they are all wrong; this was never a temple at all, it was a Council Chamber, and the very name of it, the 'Council of Penruth,' confirms that. No doubt there was a temple somewhere about; dearly should I like to find it."

It had been hot work climbing up that steep, slippery hillside from the village, and we sat down within the circle, leaning our backs against two adjacent stones, and as we sat and rested Frank explained to me the grounds of his belief.

"If you care to count them," he said, "you'll find there are twenty-one of these monoliths, against two of which you and I are leaning, and if you care to measure the distances between them you will find that they are all equal. Each stone, in fact, represents the seat of a member of the council of twenty-one. But if the place had been a temple there would have been a larger gap between two of the stones towards the east, where the gate of the temple was, facing the rising sun, and somewhere within the circle, probably exactly in the middle, there would have been a large, flat stone, which was the stone of sacrifice, where no doubt human victims were offered. Or, if the stone had disappeared, there would have been a depression where it once was. Those are the distinguishing marks of a temple, and this place lacks them. It has always been assumed that it was a temple, and it has been described as such. But I am sure I am right about it."

"But there is a temple somewhere about?" I asked.

"Certain to be. If any of these prehistoric settlements was large enough to have a council hall, it would certainly have had a temple, though the remains of it have very likely disappeared. When the country was Christianised, the old religion—if you can call it a religion—was reckoned an abomination, and the places of worship were destroyed, just as the Israelites destroyed the groves of Baal. But I mean to explore very thoroughly here: there may be remains in some of those woods down there. This is just the sort of remote place where the temple might have escaped destruction."

"And what was the ancient religion?" I asked.

"Very little is known about it. It certainly was a religion not of love but fear. The gods were the blind powers of nature, manifesting themselves in storms and destruction and plague, and had to be propitiated with human sacrifices. And the priests, of course, dealt in magic and sorcery. They were the governing class, and kept their power alive by terror. If you offended them, as likely as not you would be sent for and told that the gods required your eldest son as a blood-offering next mid-summer day at sunrise when the first beams of morning shone through the eastern gate of the temple. It was wise to be a good churchman in those days."

"It looks a kindly country nowadays," I said. "The temples of the old gods are empty."

"Yes, but it's extraordinary how old superstitions linger. It isn't a year ago that there was a witch-craft trial in Penzance. The cattle belonging to some farmer near here began to pine and die, and he went to an old woman who said that a spell had been cast on them, and that if he paid her she could remove it. He went on paying and paying, and at last got tired of that and prosecuted her instead."

He looked at his watch.

"Let's take a stroll before dinner," he said. "Instead of going back the way we came, we might make a ramble down the hillside in front and through the woods. They look rather attractive."

"And may conceal a pagan temple," said I, getting up.

We skirted the harvest fields, and found a path leading through a big fir-wood that climbed up the hillside. The trees were of no great growth as regards height, and the prevalent wind from the south-west, to which they stood exposed, had combed and pressed their branches landwards. But the foliage of the tree-tops was very dense, making a curious sombre twilight as we penetrated deeper into the wood. There was no undergrowth whatever below them, the ground was spread thick and smooth with fallen pine needles, and with the tree trunks rising straight and column-like and that thick roof of branches above, the place looked like some great hall of nature's building. No whisper of wind moved overhead, and so dark and still was it that you might easily have conceived yourself to be walking up the aisle of some walled-in place. The smell of the firs was thick in the air like incense, and the foot went noiselessly as over spread carpets. No birds flitted between the tree trunks or called to each other, the only noise was the murmurous buzz of flies, which sounded like some long-held organ note.

It had been hot enough outside in the fresh draught off the sea, but here where no breeze winnowed the air it was stiflingly close, and as we plunged deeper into the dimness I was conscious of some gathering oppression of the spirit. It was an uncomfortable place, it seemed thick with unseen presences. And the same notion must have struck Frank as well.

"I feel as if we were being watched," he said. "There are eyes peeping at us from behind the trunks, and they don't like us. Now what makes so silly an idea enter my head?"

"A grove of Baal is it?" I suggested. "One that has escaped destruction and is full of the spirits of murderous priests."

"I wish it was," he said. "Then we could inquire the way to the temple."

Suddenly he pointed ahead.

"Hullo, what's that?" he said.

I followed the direction of his finger, and for one half-second thought I saw the glimmer of something white moving among the trees. But before I could focus it it was gone. Somehow, the heat and the oppression had got on my nerves.

"Well, it's not our wood," I said. "I suppose other people have just as much right to walk here. But I've had enough of tree-trunks, I should like to have done with the wood."

Even as I spoke, I saw it was getting lighter in front of us; glimmers of day began to show between the thick-set trunks, and presently we found ourselves threading the last row of the trees. The light of day poured in again and the stir of the sea breeze; it was like coming out of some crowded and airless building into the open air.

We emerged into a delectable place; a broad stretch of downland turf was spread in front of us, smooth and ancient turf like that in the circle, jewelled with thyme and centaury and bugloss. The path we had been following lay straight across this, and dipping down over the edge of it we came suddenly on the most enchanting little house, low and two-storied, standing in a small enclosure of lawn and garden beds. The hill behind it had evidently once been quarried, but long ago, for now the sheer sides of it were overgrown with a tangle of ivy and briony, and at their base lay a pool of water. Beyond and bordering the lawn was a copse of birches and hornbeams, which half encircled the clearing in which stood house and garden. The house itself, smothered in honeysuckle and climbing fuchsia, seemed unoccupied, for the chimneys were smokeless and the blinds drawn down over the windows. As we turned the corner of its low fence and came on to the front of it, the impression was verified, for there by the gate was a notice proclaiming that it was to be let furnished, and directing that application should be made to a house agent in St. Caradoc's.

"But it's a pocket Paradise," said I. "Why shouldn't we——"

Frank interrupted me.

"Of course there's no reason why we shouldn't," he said. "In fact, there's every reason why we should. The manager at the hotel told me they were filling up next week and wanted to know for how long we should stop. We'll make inquiries to-morrow morning, and find the agent and the keys."

The keys next morning revealed a charm within that came up to the promise of what we had seen without, and, what was as wonderful, the agent could provide our staff as well. This consisted of a rotund and capable Cornishwoman who, with her daughter to help her, would arrive early every morning, and remain till she had served our dinner, and then go back to her cottage in St. Caradoc's. If that would suffice us, she was ready to be in charge as soon as we settled to take the little house; it must be understood, however, that she would not sleep there. Without making any further inquiries, the assurance that she was a clean and capable cook and competent in every way was enough, and two days afterwards we entered into possession. The rent asked was extraordinarily low, and my suspicious mind, as we went through the house, visualised an absence of water-supply or a kitchen range that, while getting red hot, left its ovens as in the chill of an Arctic night. But no such dispiriting discoveries awaited us; Mrs. Fennell turned taps and manipulated dampers, and, scouring capably through the house, pronounced on her solemn guarantee that we should be very comfortable. "But I go back to my own house at night, gentlemen," she said, "and I promise you the water will be hot and your breakfast ready for you by eight in the morning."

We entered that afternoon; our luggage had been sent up an hour before, and when we arrived the portmanteaux were already unpacked and clothes bestowed in their drawers, and tea ready in the sitting-room. It and its adjoining dining-room with a small parqueted hall, formed the ground floor accommodation. Beyond the dining-room was the kitchen, the convenience of which had already satisfied Mrs. Fennell. Upstairs there were two good bedrooms, and above the kitchen two smaller servants' rooms, which, by our arrangement, would be unoccupied. There was a bathroom between the two bedrooms with a door into it from each; for two friends occupying the house nothing could have been more exactly what was wanted with nothing to spare. Mrs. Fennell gave us an admirable plain dinner, and by nine o'clock she had locked the outer kitchen door and left us.

Before going to bed we wandered out into the garden, marvelling at our luck. The hotel, as the manager had told us, was already beginning to fill up, the dining-room to-night would have been a cackle of voices, the sitting-room crowded, and surely it was a wonderfully good exchange to be housed in this commodious little tranquillity of a place, with our own unobtrusive establishment that came at dawn and left at night. It remained only to see if this paragon who was so proficient in her kitchen would be as punctual in the morning.

"But I wonder why she and her daughter would not establish themselves here," said Frank. "They live alone down in the village. You'd have thought that they would have shut their cottage up, and saved themselves a morning and evening tramp."

"Gregariousness," said I. "They like to know that there are people, just people, close at hand and to right and left. I like to know that there are not. I like——"

As I spoke we turned at the garden gate, where the notice that the house was to let had been, and my eyes, quite idly, travelled across the space of open downland to the black fringe of the wood that stood above it, and for a moment, bright, and then quenched again like the line of fire made by a match that has been struck and has not flared, I saw a light there. It was only for a second that it was visible, but it must have been somewhere inside the wood, for against that luminous streak I saw the shape of the fir trunks.

"Did you see that?" I said to Frank.

"A light in the wood?" he asked. "Yes, it has appeared there several times. Just for a moment and then disappearing again. Some farmer, perhaps, finding his way home."

That was a very sensible conclusion, and, for some reason that I did not trouble to probe, my mind hastened to adopt it. After all, who was more likely to be passing through the wood than men from the upland farms going home at closing time from the Red Lion at St. Caradoc's?

I was roused next morning out of very deep sleep by the entry of Mrs. Fennell with hot water; it was a struggle to join myself up with the waking world again. I had the impression of having dreamed very vividly of things dark and dim, and of perilous places, and though I had certainly slept for something like eight hours at a stretch I felt curiously unrefreshed. At breakfast Frank was more silent than his wont, but presently we were making plans for the day. He proposed to explore the wood again, while I was busy with my work; in the afternoon a round of golf would bring us to teatime. Before he started and I settled down, we strolled about the garden that dozed tranquilly in the hot morning sun, and again congratulated ourselves on our exchange from the hotel. We went down to the pool below the quarried cliff, and there I left him to return to the house, while he, in order to start exploring at once, followed an overgrown path that led into the copse of birch and hornbeam of which I have spoken. But I had not crossed the lawn before I heard myself called.

"Come here a minute," he shouted, "I've found something interesting." I retraced my steps, and pushing through the trees found him standing by a tall, black granite stone that pushed its moss-green head above the undergrowth.

"It's a monolith," he said excitedly. "It's like one of those stones in the circle. Perhaps there has been another circle here, or, perhaps, it's a stone of the temple. It's deep in the earth, it looks as if it was in place. Let's see if we can find another in this copse."

He pushed on into the thick growing trees to the right of the path, and I, infected with his enthusiasm, made an exploration to the left. Before long I came upon another stone of the same character as the first, and my shout of discovery was echoed by his. Yet another rewarded his hunting, and as I emerged from the copse on the edge of the quarry pool I found a fifth, standing but fallen forward in a bed of rushes that fringed the water.

In the excitement of this find, my planned studiousness was, of course, abandoned; so, too, when we had eaten a hearty lunch, was the projected game of golf, and before evening we had arrived at a rough scheme of the entire place. Most of the stones were in the belt of copse that half-encircled the house, and with a tape-measure we found that these were set at uniform intervals from each other except that exactly twice that interval separated the two stones that lay due east of the circle. In the bank that lay to the south of the house several were missing, but in each case, by digging at the proper intervals, we found fragments of granite grassed over in the soil, which indicated that these stones had been broken up and used, probably, for building materials, and this conjecture of Frank's was confirmed by the discovery of pieces of granite built into the walls of the house we occupied.

He had jotted down the approximate position of the stones, and passed over to me the paper on which he had drawn his plan.

"Without doubt it's a temple," he said, "there's the double interval at the east, which I told you about, and which was the gate into it."

I looked at what he had drawn.

"Then our house stands just in the centre of it," I said.

"Yes; what vandals they were to build it just there," said he. "Probably the stone of sacrifice lies somewhere below it. Good Lord, dinner ready, Mrs. Fennell? I had no idea it was so late."

The sky had clouded over during the afternoon, and while we sat at dinner, a windless and heavy rain began to fall and thunder to mutter over the sea. Mrs. Fennell came in to enquire into our tastes for to-morrow, and as there was every appearance of a violent storm approaching, I asked her whether she and her girl would not stop here for the night and save themselves a wetting.

"No, I'll be off now, sir, thank you," she said. "We don't mind a wetting in Cornwall."

"But not very good for your rheumatism," I said. She had mentioned that she was a sufferer in this respect.

A blink of lightning flashed rather vividly across the uncurtained windows, and the rain hissed more heavily.

"No, I'll be off now," she said, "for it's late already. Good night, gentlemen."

We heard her turn the key in the kitchen door, and presently the figures of herself and her girl passed the window.

"Not even umbrellas," said Frank. "They'll be drenched before they get down."

"I wonder why they wouldn't stop," said I.

Frank was soon employed on preparations for a plan to scale that he was meaning to make to-morrow, and he began putting in the house, which he had ascertained stood just in the centre of the temple. The size of the ground plan of it was all he required on the scale he intended for the complete plan, and after measuring the sitting-room, passage, and dining-room, he went through into the kitchen. Meanwhile, I had settled down to the work I had intended to do this morning, and proposed to get a couple of solid hours at it before I went to bed. It was rather hard to get the thread of it again, and for some time I floundered with false starts and erased sentences, but before long I got into better form, and was already happily absorbed in it when he called me from the kitchen.

"Oh, I can't come," I said, "I'm busy."

"Just a moment, please," he shouted.

I laid down my pen and went to him. He had moved the kitchen table aside and turned up the drugget that covered the floor.

"Look there!" he said.

The floor was paved with stone of the district, very likely from the quarry just outside. But in the centre was an oblong slab of granite, some six feet by four in dimensions.

"That's a whacking big stone," I said. "Odd of them to have been at the trouble of putting that there."

"They didn't," said he. "I'll bet it was there when they laid the floor!"

Then I understood.

"The stone of sacrifice?" I asked.

"Rather. Granite and just in the centre of the temple. It can't be anything else."

Some sudden thrill of horror seized me. It was on that stone that young boys and maidens, torn from their mother's arms and bound hand and foot, were laid, while the priest, with one hand over the victim's eyes, plunged the flint knife into the smooth, white throat, sawing through the tissue till the blood spurted from the severed artery.... In the flickering light of the candle Frank carried the stone seemed wet and darkly glistening, and was that noise only the rain volleying on the roof, or the beating of drums to drown the cries of the victim?...

"It's terrible," I said. "I wish you hadn't found it."

Frank was on his knees by it, examining the surface of it. "I can't say I agree with you," he said. "It just puts the final touch of certainty on my discovery. Besides, whether I had found it or not, it would have been there just the same."

"Well, I'm going on with my work," I said. "It's more cheerful than stones of sacrifice."

He laughed.

"I hope it's as interesting," he said.

It appeared, when I went back to it, that it was not, and try as I would I could not recapture the interest which is necessary to production of any kind. Even my eye wandered from the words I wrote; as for my mind, it would give only the most cursory glance at that for which I demanded its fixed attention. It was busy elsewhere. I found myself, at its bidding, scrutinizing the shadowy corners of the room, but there was nothing there, and all the time some strange darkness, blacker than that which pressed in upon the house, began to grow upon my spirit. There was fear mingled with it, though I did not know what I was afraid of, but chiefly it was some sort of despair and depression, distant as yet and undefined, but quietly closing in upon me.... As I sat with my pen still in my hand, trying to analyse these perturbed and troubled sensations, I heard Frank call out sharply from the kitchen, the door of which, on my return, I had left open.

"Hullo!" he cried. "What's that? Is anyone there?"

I jumped from my seat and went to join him. He was standing close to the stove, holding his candle above his head, and looking at the door into the garden, which Mrs. Fennell had locked on her departure.

"What's the matter?" I asked.

He looked round at me, startled by the sound of my voice.

"Curious," he said, "I was just measuring the stone, when out of the corner of my eye I thought I saw that door open. But it's locked, isn't it?"

He tried the handle, but sure enough it was locked.

"Optical delusion," he said. "Well, I've finished here for the present. But what a night! Frightfully oppressive, isn't it? And not a breath of air stirring."

We went back to the sitting-room. I put away my laboured manuscript and we got out the cards for a game of piquet. But after one _partie_, he rose with a yawn.

"I really don't think I could keep awake for another," he said, "I'm heavy with sleep. Let's have a breath of air, the rain seems to have stopped, and go to bed. Or are you going to sit up and work?"

I had not meant to do so, but his suggestion made me determine to have another try. There was certainly some mysterious pall of depression on me, and the wisest thing to do was to fight it.

"I shall try for half an hour," I said, "and see how it goes," and I followed him to the front door of the house. The rain, as he said, had ceased, but the darkness was impenetrable, and shuffling with our feet, we took a few steps along the gravel path to the corner of the house. There the light from the sitting-room windows cast a circle of illumination, and one could see the flower-beds glistening with the wet. Though it was night, the air was still so hot that the gravel path was steaming. Beyond that nothing was visible of the lawn or the hill that sloped up to the fir-wood. But, as we stood there, I saw, as last night, a light moving up there. Now, however, it seemed to be outside the wood, for its progress was not interrupted by the tree-trunks.

Frank saw it too, and pointed at it.

"It's too wet to-night," he said, "but to-morrow evening, I vote we go up there, and see who these nightly wanderers are. It's coming closer, and there's another of them."

Even as we looked a third light sprang up, and in another moment all had vanished again.

I carried out my intention of trying to work, but I could make nothing of it, and presently I found myself nodding over a page that contained nothing but erasures. With head bent forward, I drifted into a doze and from dozing into sleep, and when I woke I found the lamp burning low and the wick smouldering. I seemed to have come back from some very distant place, and, only half awake, I lit a candle and quenched the lamp and went to the windows to bolt them. And then my heart stood still, for I thought I saw someone standing outside and looking in through the intervening glass. But it must have been a sleepy fancy, for now, broad awake again, I was staring at my own reflection cast by the candle on the window. I told myself that what I had seen was no more than that, but as I creaked my way upstairs I found myself asking if I really believed that....

As I dressed next morning, after another long but unrefreshing night, I began puzzling over a lost memory to which I had tried to find the clue yesterday. There was a bookcase in the sitting-room with some two or three dozen volumes in it, and opening one or two of these I had found the name Samuel Townwick inscribed in them. I knew I had seen that name not so many months ago in the daily Press, but I could not recapture the connection in which I had read it; but from the recurrence of it in these books it was reasonable to conjecture that he was the owner of the house we occupied. In taking it, his name had not come up; the house agent had plenary powers, and our deposit of a fortnight's rent clinched the contract. But this morning the name still haunted me, and since I had other small businesses in St. Caradoc's, I settled to walk down there and make some definite inquiry at the agent's. Frank was too busy with his plan to accompany me, and I set out alone.

The feeling of depression and vague foreboding was more leaden than ever this morning, and I was aware by that sixth sense, which needs no speech or language, that he was a prey to the same causeless weight. But I had not gone fifty yards from the house when the burden of it was lifted from me, and I knew again the exhilaration proper to such a morning. The rain of last evening had cleared the air, the sea breeze drew lightly landwards and, as if I had come out of some tunnel, I rejoiced in the morning splendour. The village hummed with holiday: Mr. Cranston received me with polite enquiries as to our comfort and Mrs. Fennell's capability, and having assured him on that score, I approached my point.

"Mr. Samuel Townwick is the owner, is he not?" I asked.

The agent's smile faded a little.

"He was, sir," he said. "I act for the executors."

Suddenly, in a flash, some of what I had been groping for came back to me. "I begin to remember," I said. "He died suddenly; there was an inquest. I want to know the rest. Hadn't you better tell me?"

He shifted his glance and came back to me again.

"It was a painful affair," he said. "The executors naturally do not want it talked about."

Another glimpse of what I had forgotten blinked on my memory.

"Suicide," I said. "The usual verdict of unsound mind was brought in. And—and is that why Mrs. Fennell won't sleep in the house? She left last night in a deluge of rain."

I readily gave him my promise of secrecy, for I had not the slightest desire to tell Frank, and he told me the rest. Mr. Townwick had been for some days in a very depressed state of mind, and one morning the servants coming down had found him lying underneath the kitchen table with his throat cut. Beside him was a sharp, curiously-shaped fragment of flint covered with blood. The jagged nature of the wound had confirmed the idea that he had sawn at his throat till he had severed the jugular vein. Murder was ruled out, for he was a strong man, and there were no marks on his body or about the room of there having been any struggle, nor any sign of an assailant having entered. Both kitchen doors were locked on the inside, his valuables were untouched, and from the position of the body the only reasonable inference was that he had laid down under the table, and there deliberately done himself to death…. I repeated my assurance of silence and went out.

I knew now what the source of my nameless horror and depression had been. It was no haunting spectre of Townwick that I feared; it was the power, whatever that was, which had driven him to kill himself on the stone of sacrifice.

I went back up the hill: there was the garden blazing in the July noon, and the sweet tranquillity of the place was spread abroad in the air. But I had no sooner passed the copse and come within the circle than the dead weight of something unseen began to lay its burden on me again. There _was_ something here, horrible and menacing and potent.

I found Frank in the sitting-room. His head was bent over his plan, and he started as I entered.

"Hullo!" he said. "I've made all my measurements and I want to sit tight and finish my plan to-day. I don't know why, but I feel I must hurry about it and get it done. And I've got the most awful fit of the blues. I can't account for it, but anyhow, occupation is the best thing. Go in to lunch, will you, I don't want any."

I looked at him and saw some indefinable change had come over his face. There was terror in his eyes that came from within: I can express it in no other way than that.

"Anything wrong?" I asked.

"No; just blues. I want to go on working. This evening, you know, we have to see where those lights come from."

All afternoon he sat close over his work, and it was not till the day was fading that he got up.

"That's done," he said. "Good Lord, we have found a temple and a half! And I'm horribly tired. I shall have a snooze till dinner."

The invasion of fear beleaguered me, it seemed to pour in through the open windows in the gathering dusk, it gathered its reinforcements outside, ready to support the onrush of it. And yet how childish it was to yield to it. By now we were alone in the house, for we had told Mrs. Fennell that a cold meal would serve us in this heat, and while Frank slept I had heard the lock of the outside kitchen door turn and she and the girl went by the window.

Presently he stirred and awoke. I had lit the lamp, and I saw his hand feel in his waistcoat pocket, and he drew out a small object which he held out to me.

"A flint knife," he said. "I picked it up in the garden this morning. It's got a fine edge to it."

At that I felt a prickle of terror run through the hair of my head, and I jumped up.

"Look here," I said, "you've had no walk to-day, and that always gives you the blues. Let's go down and dine at the hotel."

His head was outside the illumination of the lamp, and from the dimness there came a curious cackle of laughter.

"But I can't," he said. "How strange that you don't know that I can't. They've surrounded the place, and there's no way out. Listen! Can't you hear the drums and the squeal of their pipes? And their hands are about me. Christ! It's terrible to die."

He got up and began to move with curious little shuffling steps towards the kitchen. I had laid the flint knife down on the table and he snatched it up. The horror of presences unseen and multitudinous closed in round me, but I knew they were concentrated not on me, but on him. They poured in, not through the window alone but through the solid walls of the house; outside on the lawn there were lights moving, slow and orderly.

I had still control of my mind, the awfulness and the imminence of what so closely beset us gave me the courage and clearness of despair. I darted from my chair and stood with my back to the kitchen door.

"You're not to go in there," I said. "You must come away with me out of this. Pull yourself together, Frank. We'll get through yet; once outside the garden we're safe."

He paid no attention to what I said; it was as if he did not hear me. He laid his hand on my shoulder, and I felt his fingers press through the muscles and grind like points of steel on the underlying bone. Some maniac force possessed them, and he pulled me aside as if I had been a feather.

There was one thing only to be done. With my disengaged arm I hit him full on the chin, and he fell like a log across the floor. Without pausing for a second I gripped him round the knees and began dragging him senseless and inert towards the door.

It is difficult to state in words what those next few minutes held. I saw nothing. I heard nothing. I felt no touch of invisible hands upon me, but I can imagine no grinding agony of pain that wrenches body and soul asunder to equal that war of the evil and the unseen that raged about me. I struggled against no visible adversary, and there was the horror of it, for I am sure that no phantom of the dead that die not could have evoked so unnerving a terror.

Before those intangible hosts had fully closed in round me and my unconscious burden, I had got him on to the lawn, and it was then that the full stress of their beleaguering might poured in upon me. Strange fugitive lights wavered round me and muttered voices filled the air, and as I dragged Frank over the grass his weight seemed to grow till it was not a man's body that I was pulling along, but something well-nigh immovable, so that I had to tug and pant for breath and tug again.

"God help us both," I heard myself muttering. "Deliver us from our ghostly enemies ..." and again I tugged and panted for breath. Close at hand now was the ring of enclosing copse, where the stones of the circle stood, and I made one final effort of concentration, for I knew that my spirit was spent, and soon there would be no power of fight left in me at all.

"In the name of the Holiest, and by the power of the Highest," I cried aloud, and waited for a moment, gathering what dregs of strength were still left in me. And then I leaned forward, and the strained sinews of my legs were slackened as the weight of Frank's body moved after me, and I made another step, and yet another, and we had passed beyond the copse, and out of the accursed precinct.

I knew no more after that. I had fallen forwards half across him, and when I regained my senses he was stirring, and the dew of the grass was on my face. There stood the house, with the lamp still burning in the window of the sitting-room, and the quiet night was around us, with a clear and starry heaven.

THE END

Printed in Great Britain
by Amazon

55977608R00078